UNMASK

BOOK 3

TAKING THE NEXT STEP

A Novel By

CALENTHIA YVETTE MILLER

I

A'Lure Publishing, LLC

UNMASK- Book 3 Taking The Next Step©2023

By Calenthia Yvette Miller

Illustration by: Anthony L. Wardrett

Worldloveart@gmail.com

Instagram @worldloveart

For Information Contact:

Info@alurepublishingllc.com

Alurepublishingllc.com

Canvasofthoughts. Shop

DEDICATION

This book is dedicated to the millions of people who have yet to tap into their hidden gifts.
"Masterpieces are constructed by those who dare to dream beyond the simple word NO."
Dr. Calenthia Yvette Miller

CONTENTS

PROLOGUE

Royce gazed at the letter; his mind consumed by thoughts of his recent conversation with Bryce while they awaited Mia's arrival. Despite his excitement at the prospect of fatherhood, he secretly harbored no desire to co-parent with Bria. However, his reservations vanished upon seeing Mia with the clinical response team. All he wanted was to hold and safeguard her. Royce was overcome with emotion as he reviewed the results for the tenth time, questioning how this could happen again, first with Skylar and now with Bria. He couldn't help but wonder how much more he could withstand.

He was utterly overwhelmed by heartbreak and couldn't regain his composure. He finally broke down and let out all of the sorrows, disappointments, and misfortunes he had been holding in over the past year, and he buried his head in Anya's waiting arms.

Anya knew what Royce was feeling at that moment as she had experienced that same hurt many times. Anya's thoughts returned to a time when her life was simple. A time when there were no worries in the world. It was a time when you just had fun being a kid, free to enjoy and explore the unknown. Anya walked Royce to her car, opened the passenger door, waited for him to get in, and drove home.

As Anya parked the car on the rooftop, the view of tonight's river seemed more picturesque and peaceful. This is just what they both needed: serenity. The ripple of the waves glided against the massive rocks, causing a small explosion of water to cascade into the air. As the water gradually fell, Anya realized that our lives were similar, like the river. Sometimes, our life is smooth like a current, taking us on an unknown journey with purpose. But other times, it is relentless and unbearable to navigate. Tonight was one of those times; the river was like a beast bearing down on our back, ready to sweep us under. Anya intertwined her fingers with Royce's as they sat quietly, appreciating the captivating beauty of nature unfolding in front of them.

It was after one in the morning when Anya and Royce entered the house. Royce still had yet to say anything. He headed to the living room and stretched out on the oversized couch. Meanwhile, Anya hurried to the bathroom before heading to the kitchen to satisfy her hunger. It had been hours since she last ate, and she craved the homemade cream cheese Danish that Mrs. Margaret had gifted her. Anya often had a sweet tooth, which signaled her impending monthly cycle. While she usually managed her symptoms, last month was an entirely different story.

On the first day, severe cramps kept her bedridden, making her migraines feel like a walk in the park. Royce grew concerned and suggested a trip to the emergency room, but Anya convinced him otherwise. Fortunately, he stayed home to care for her instead. This is why she appreciated and loved this man. Anya placed the Danish on a plate, grabbed her tea and a can of Dr. Pepper from the refrigerator, and headed into the living room.

Royce was still lying on the couch, looking bewildered. Anya placed the pastry and soda on the end table and retreated to the sofa. After Anya finished the Danish and tea, she felt herself getting sleepy. When she opened her eyes again, the sun slowly appeared through the blinds, indicating a new day. Royce was standing at the window, looking out. Anya walked up behind him, wrapped her arms around his trim waistline, and rested her head in the middle of his lower back.

Royce turned and faced Anya and said," I love you, Anya McMichael and no other man will ever love you as much as I do. I am unsure what these next few days or months will be like, especially after receiving such devastating news. But please promise me that you will never keep anything from me". Anya nodded her head in agreement. Royce kissed her, and that kiss was different from all the others. Was it because of the results he had just received, or was it something else?

Chapter 1
NEW TERRITORY

Royce had just left court when Anya called. Hello beautiful. Hi handsome. Are you on your way home?

"Yes, I should be there in about twenty minutes," Royce answered.

"Great. Can you stop and pick up something for dinner?" Anya asked.

"Absolutely. What do you want to eat?" Royce inquired.

"You pick," Anya said.

"OK, see you shortly," Royce said before hanging up. He quickly made a mental note to swing by their favorite restaurant on the way home.

UNMASK

A lot has occurred in the past year. Royce and Anya now live together at her place. After discovering the paternity test results, Royce sold the house he shared with Skylar to Mr. Overton. He and Bryce are completing the first phase of constructing affordable homes for first-time buyers. Royce also transformed his condo into an Air BNB and is converting the remaining space downstairs into one or two-bedroom suites, potentially with a small restaurant in the back of the building.

Anya returned to work part-time and helped at the boutique with Mrs. Margaret at least twice weekly. She sees Ocean occasionally when she comes in and works with her great-grandmother. Sebastián and Anya are still friends, and they finally had the opportunity to clear the air between them.

Royce arrived home with Thai food for dinner and found that Anya had planned a special evening for them. The aroma of lilac and jasmine filled the house while candles illuminated their cozy setup. Soft jazz music played in the background as Royce entered the living room. Curious about the surprise, he asked Anya what was going on. She revealed they were in for a romantic night together and guided him to the blanket where the fruit and wine awaited. Anya removed Royce's jacket and kissed him tenderly before inviting him to sit. She then prepared his plate while Royce settled in.

It has been over four months, and this is the first time the house has been this quiet. Anya said," Royce agreed with her. We have been going non-stop with our businesses expanding and the pending relocation to Miami.

How was your day? Anya asked.

Good. My caseload has significantly been reduced since the firm hired Chris to replace me when we moved. Chris is a great guy and a wonderful friend to you. Yes, he is. I just got off the phone with him, and he informed me that Lucas was found guilty of all charges, while Bria had her charges dropped before the trial.

After discovering that Nate was Mia's father, Bria relocated to a different state with the baby. Royce receives occasional updates from Kane about Mia's well-being. Anya was aware of Royce's disappointment that Mia was not his child. It is important to note that Mia is a lovely baby, and Royce would have made an excellent father. However, I would never have asked Royce to choose between me and his child. But that Bria is messy.

Royce offered Anya a glass of wine and proposed a toast to new beginnings and opportunities for their future. And sleepless nights, Anya replied. CHEERS! Royce questioned Anya, "Are you implying something, Ms. McMichael?" In response, Mr. Blackmon asked, "What exactly are you insinuating?" Nothing.

But I do know what I want for dessert. And what might that be? Come here and let me tell you in your ear.

Anya rose from the blanket and walked the short distance to Royce. Anya leaned in, and the rich, baritone voice echoed in her ear as he said, "I need YOU just like I need air to breathe." Royce placed soft kisses along Anya's neck. When Royce got to Anya's ear, she melted like butter. His kisses were strategically aimed in the areas that caused Anya to lose her mind. Royce slowly removed the turquoise and black form-fitting knitted dress that Anya wore. She stood there in only her matching silver lace bra and panties. Anya immediately wrapped her arms around herself to hide the imperfections.

Royce guided her hands away from her body. 'DO YOU KNOW YOU ARE A BEAUTIFUL QUEEN"? You are perfect in every way, and I promise to show and tell you that every day of your life.

After a long night of lovemaking, Royce was up and out of the house before eight that morning. Unfortunately, Anya did not have that same stamina and remained in bed until ten. The phone rang; it was the real estate broker Terri. Anya had been talking with Terri long-distance for the past six months, trying hard to locate a property that would serve as their next satellite office. The firm had done exceptionally well despite the lingering effects of COVID.

They had increased their profit margin by seventy-seven percent, twelve percent above what had been forecasted.

Good morning, Anya: I hope I did not wake you. No, Terri, you did not, Anya said. I sent you some more properties last night. I am very excited about a property that still needs to be listed in your desired area, the Art District. You should see it. When does it go on the market? In a week, Terri advised. Anya opened the text and immediately fell in love with the building when she saw the pictures. The 35,000-square-foot three-story Art Deco building was astonishing. Terri, can you schedule some time for me to view the property on Saturday? Before ending the call, Anya confirmed the asking price and any potential red flags that could delay the closing if she decided to purchase the property. Terri indicated no but advised that she would contact the seller to confirm the property's status.

Anya was excited about how things were going in her personal and professional life. Last night was incredible, as always. Royce was so attentive to her needs and was always gentle with her. But sometimes, she wished Royce would stop handling her with kid gloves; even after her last appointment with Dr. Summerton, Royce wanted to make sure he asked about their intimate activities. Dr. Summerton assured Royce that engaging in sexual intercourse helps reduce stress and depression, lowers a woman's risk of heart attacks, and reduces pain.

In addition, research has shown that during sex, our bodies release a hormone called endorphins. Endorphins act as our natural pain reliever. This will help since she suffers from migraines and frequent headaches. Anya knows Royce has the best intentions for her, but she wants to experience that unadulterated passion she had read about in Zane's and Brenda Jackson's books. Anya knows she loved and adored Royce and couldn't imagine her life without him. But she was not someone to sit idle and do nothing. Anya knew just what she needed to do.

The elevator opened on the sixth floor. Anya stepped off and saw her firm's name on the door; she became emotional. This journey, she knows, has been a testament to her faith and determination to succeed. But most of all, the promise she made to her father was never to give up.

Anya entered the suite and was greeted by Stacie and Erin. Erin was new to the firm's family. Three months ago, Erin was hired as a receptionist to support Stacie with calls and additional tasks due to the increased number of new clients. Stacie reminded Anya that she had two interviews on the calendar today and placed their resumes on her desk to review. Anya bypassed her office and headed toward the conference room. And as she expected, Leah was there. Anya hugged Leah and said good morning. Do you and Bryce have any plans this weekend? Anya asked. Leah replied no. Bryce is away on business in Arizona until next week. Do you want to go with me to Miami to look at some potential office space? Of course, I would. This will give me a chance to get some more authentic Cuban food.

Anya laughed. I cannot help it; Marisol has spoiled me, and I am now hooked. Leah said—no need to explain. I can go for a Cuban sandwich right now myself. I will have Stacie make our flight reservations. What about Royce? Is he not going? I have not told him. Terri called me this morning, and he had already gone to the office. I will call him after these interviews to let him know. Plus, it gives us a chance to spend some girl time together. Have you looked at the resumes of the candidates? No, I have not. Stacie put them on my desk so we could review them together. After the interviews, Anya called Royce, and her call went to voicemail. She left him a message and headed to lunch with the team.

Chapter 2

GREAT ADVENTURE

Sebastián had shaken hands and greeted so many people in the last two hours that he had forgotten many of their names. Ocean was being inducted into the National Honor and Presidential Scholar Society tonight. This was extra special because she would be the first to achieve this accolade as a junior and, more importantly, a female of color at a predominately European school. Sebastian was so proud of his baby girl. She is truly making her mark in the world.

Sebastian is equally grateful for her support tonight from Ocean's grandparents, Pop and Ma Franklin, Mrs. Margaret, Ja'Nae, and Marisa's parents, Joyce and Anderson. Unfortunately, Artisan still could not travel, and Mrs. Sylvie opted to stay by his side as he recovered.

However, Ocean was able to video chat with them last night. The expression on Artisan's face was priceless as Ocean and he talked; it filled Sebastian's heart with so much joy. Sadly, Marisa was not in attendance either, as she was on assignment in London covering a story on the Prime Minister. Sebastian promised Marisa he would capture everything on video and send it to her. Ocean was asked to give the open remarks for tonight's event. Sebastián escorted Ocean to the podium, kissed her cheek, and told her how proud he was of her accomplishment. Then, Ocean poised herself, took a deep breath, and began.

"It is an honor to be the recipient of such prestigious awards. If I could be transparent, I had initially declined to give this speech. But, after my conversation with a sagacious man I met at the library, I reconsidered. He said that, as people, we have the opportunity to make many mistakes throughout our lives. But the real opportunity comes when we can turn those mistakes into purpose.

So, what is my purpose? To change the world? Or is it to eliminate world hunger? Those things are great but also cliché. I aim to change the narrative of girls and boys who look like me. To show the world that our diverse backgrounds and heritage remind us that we descend from the royalty that built this country.

But society has birthed this outlandish idea that we are lazy and will never amount to anything. So, my purpose today is to honor my ancestors, who have paved the way for me to stand here tonight.

I boldly claim the lies formed in the closed minds of so many long ago are no longer a narrative I subscribe to. My purpose is that many more like me will have the opportunity to stand in this same spot for years to come." Ocean graciously thanked the audience, and before leaving the podium, she received a standing ovation that lasted for over two minutes.

As Sebastian looked around, there was no dry eye in the room, including his. He could not be prouder of Ocean than he was at that moment. The program ended at about eight, and we headed home.

Sebastián decided to stay in the city and take the drive to the country in the morning. As he headed down Interstate 40, he reflected on everything that had happened in twelve months. He had flown back with Ja'Nae to Paris after ensuring Margaret was good after being released from the hospital. The doctor said Margaret had passed out from exhaustion. This was the day he saw Ja'Nae for the first time since he was ten.

Once in Paris, he met Mrs. J. They also flew to London and spent time with his grandfather Artisan, Mrs. Sylvie, Artie, Daphanie, Jocelyn, Stuart, and his son Cameron. Ja'Nae and I are still a work in progress, but not what it once was.

Like any relationship, it takes time to grow and mature, which I have over the last year. Marisa and I have decided to continue to co-parent Ocean under one roof. I finally took them to the house in the country, and we moved in a week before Thanksgiving.

We all gathered at the farmhouse that Thanksgiving, and Ma and Mr. Thomas argued over who made the better bread pudding. It was Mr. Thomas, but I would not dare tell her. When I told Ma and Pop that I was their biological grandson, you would have thought they would have been surprised. Pop said," I knew you were ours because you have the same birthmark on your lower back as Leo and me. That was not a coincidence, and your mannerism was like a Franklin. You love hard and work harder to protect the ones you love." Ma and Pop have since talked with Ja'Nae, and they reassured her that they did not harbor any ill feelings toward her and understood why she did what she did.

Sebastian also has developed an excellent relationship with Margaret. He now sees where Ja'Nae and he get their stubbornness from. That Caribbean momma don't take any mess. Like Ma, she will fuss you out and ask if you want something to eat in the same breath. Sebastian now knows what it's like to feel almost complete.

Sebastián pulled his car into the driveway. He had kept the house in the city as it was a job requirement, and it was ideal if he did not want to drive the long distance to the farmhouse in the country. Ocean decided to stay at Charlie's home tonight.

Sebastián took his coat off and hung it in the closet in the foyer. He climbed the stairs to the primary bedroom and headed for the shower. He lowered his head and closed his eyes, allowing the hot water to massage the back of his neck.

Pictures of Anya invaded his mind. He could not get her out of his head. He was good after he cleared the air with Anya regarding their relationship last year. At least, that is what he told himself. The chemistry between them was electrifying.

Whenever he saw her, he wanted to take her in his arms and not let her go. He knows this will not happen because she is now in a relationship with Royce. And she says she is in love with him. Suppose he had only told her how he felt. Sebastián finished showering and went to bed.

The following morning, Sebastián decided to forgo the gym and head out early to miss the morning traffic. Marissa called after she received the footage of Ocean's speech. Sebastian could hear the excitement and the disappointment in Marisa's voice. Yet, his thoughts were still on Anya. He needs to clear his mind.

Placing his helmet and sunglasses on, he put Luke in gear and headed out. The fresh, crisp morning air was just what Sebastián needed. As he rode, he could still feel Anya's head against his back and the smell of the coconut and pineapple shampoo that danced off the curly locks of her hair. He felt his heart racing so fast he thought he was having a heart attack. How and why has he allowed Anya to affect him in such a profound way after so long? Sebastián pulled up to the farmhouse. Dialing in the code, the black iron gate opened, allowing him access to the property. Sebastián had the gate installed right before Marisa and Ocean moved in. He was promoted to the Special Investigation Unit last year, and the job required long hours and much travel; Sebastian needed to know that his girls were safe when he was away.

He parked Luke on the circular paver driveway in front of the newly renovated rustic dual staircase, giving the house an elegant look. Sebastian walked to the enclosed pasture on the property. He placed his foot against the fence and gazed at the open field. He needed to talk to Anya and tell her how he truly felt. He pulled his cell phone from the inner pocket of his leather jacket. Just as he dialed Anya's number, she was calling him.

Chapter 3

STOP

Royce had made it to work after stopping to grab him some breakfast and a cup of coffee. Last night was terrific, as always. But he knew if he did not leave this morning, he would not have. Anya's body is a work of art; I am her Picasso. I want to leave my signature on her every chance I get.

Royce knew Dr. Summerton had given them the green light to indulge in as much sex as they liked, but he was still cautious about Anya's aneurysm. Royce wanted to take their lovemaking to another level but was too scared. Chris had walked into Royce's office and sat in the chair before the desk. Hey, good morning, Chris. What's on your mind? Royce was not expecting Chris to be in the office this early. Royce, my apologies. Good morning. I just came in here unannounced. Man, no worries. What's up? Chris handed Royce the paper that was in his hand.

Mr. Chris Calloway,

My name is Dominique A. Sanchez, ESQ. I represent Nate White in a pending paternity and custody case for Mia Renee Royalty Gregory, the minor child in question. Mr. White has brought forth allegations that the child is not biologically his. He asked that the paternity test be retaken to solidify his claims that he could not father a child due to a medical procedure before marriage. In addition, there is evidence that the previously received samples may have been tampered with. Your client Royce Blackmon was initially named as one of the potential fathers in this case. Mr. Blackmon is asked to have a new sample recollected and resubmit for paternity testing on: Friday, April 16, 10:00 am Coventry Memorial Hospital Outpatient Laboratory Suite 308, 4th Floor.

Royce just looked at the paper and shook his head in disbelief. This is a recurring nightmare. I thought this chapter in my life was over. But here we are, reliving it again a year later. Royce recalls meeting with Nate, advising that he had a vasectomy before marrying Bria. Does Nate have proof that the vasectomy was fail-proof because the last test indicated he was the father? And what evidence do they have that shows the previous sample was tampered with?

Chris veered up at Royce, looking just as shocked as he was. Royce said, "I need clarification because my test was performed at a private diagnostic center. How can this be possible? Man, when I received this mail today, I headed here to tell you. I have been trying to contact the opposing attorney but have not heard back from her. But that is a question that I aim to get answered. Do you think Bria had anything to do with this, especially since she knows you are now with Anya? Royce thought about what Chris had said. Would Bria do something so spiteful just to hurt me? Royce reflected on the quote, "Hurt people hurt people. "Chris, I would not put anything past either one of them. However, I am more concerned about Mia. What if she is mine? That would mean I have missed out on all of her first milestones in her life.

Chris left Royce, giving him the space to process this news. Chris called Ms. Sanchez's office, and still no answer. Finally, he looked at the address and knew exactly where it was. Chris took the twenty-minute ride to the office. The surroundings were familiar because he had rented his first apartment about three blocks from there. Chris could still smell the aroma of the freshly baked bread from Mr. Soriano's bakery and the homemade churros that Miguel and his grandfather Pedro would sell every weekend from the window of their conversion van.

The area has since changed. The old bakery has been converted into a coffee shop with a studio apartment above it. And the Ma and Pop shops have been replaced with upscale fashion boutiques and art galleries.

Chris dialed the number once more before he got out of the car, and still, no answer. So, finally, he approached the door just as a male exited. Chris walked to the receptionist's desk and waited for someone to come. He stood there for about ten minutes, and finally, a woman appeared down the hall. Good morning. I am looking for Ms. Sanchez. Who is asking? Chris Calloway. Mr. Calloway, Dominique is not here. She had a debriefing and will not be back until later today. Chris gave the receptionist his business card and left. As he reached his car, he called the number again, and a female answered. Hello, law office of Dominique Sanchez; this is Dominique. How can I help you?

Chris could not comprehend why Ms. Sanchez would pretend to be the receptionist. He could only surmise that she was trying to hide something. So, he remained in front of the business to see if the person representing herself as the receptionist would leave. As he guessed, the mysterious woman exited the building around one o'clock; he assumed to grab lunch. Chris decided to follow her. And when the car finally stopped, he was astonished at what he saw.

Chapter 4

UNEXPECTED

Bryce had checked into his suite at The Phoenician. He was exhausted. His connecting flight in Dallas was delayed due to mechanical issues. Therefore, he missed the appointment with the city inspector. Bryce called Leah to tell her he had made it safely to Arizona.

His next call was to Sal. Hello, my friend. I see that you made it. Yes, after being delayed for two hours. Let me settle in, shower, and we can meet for dinner at seven. Bryce had to remember the two-hour time difference between Tennessee and Arizona.

Bryce showered and took a power nap before meeting with Sal. The phone rang. It was the front desk calling to wake him up. Bryce was casually dressed in khaki slacks, a salmon short-sleeve collar shirt, and loafers. As he walked to the hotel restaurant, the temperature outside was still humid at seven at night.

Bryce spotted Sal at the bar. He conversed with the bartender and an attractive woman sitting beside him. When Sal saw Bryce, he stood to greet him. It is good to see you, my friend. Sal asked what Bryce was drinking and introduced him to the woman sitting at the bar.

Bryce, this is my cousin Lourdes Vincente. We call her Lou. It is a pleasure to meet you, Mrs. Vincente. Likewise, but it's Ms. Vincente. My apologies, Bryce said. Lou took a sip of her drink and eyeballed Bryce for several seconds. Sal handed Bryce the glass of Patron, and the waiter escorted them to their table.

Bryce walked behind Ms. Vincente as they made their way to their table. She walked with confidence. Her shoulders relaxed as she took each step as if on a mission. Her attire was Bohemian-inspired. She wore a long, multicolored maxi dress and strapless sandals. Her hair was pulled up in a loose bun, revealing a white hummingbird tattooed on the back of her neck.

Once seated, Sal began talking. For the first minute, Bryce had no clue what he had said. He was transfixed by the beautiful Latina placed directly in front of him. That was not until Sal asked Bryce's opinion about the property. Bryce quickly refocused his attention on the conversation. Sal advised that he had rescheduled the inspection for tomorrow afternoon. Ms. Vincente said the realtor would meet with us on Sunday. Bryce did not realize she would join Sal and him on this business trip. Lou glanced up at Bryce to see his reaction to her last statement.

His facial expressions had not changed. She was curious about what Sal had said about her role in the business and why she was here. After being served dinner and the plan was mapped out for the rest of the week, Bryce said good night, leaving Sal and Lou at the table.

Bryce decided to take a stroll on the grounds of the property. The views of the mountains were spectacular. The state's rich history could be told by looking at the different rock formations. Bryce relaxed by the pool as he watched the sunset behind the ridge in the distance.

Then, his phone rang; it was Royce. Bryce could immediately hear the distress in his voice. Hey B, what's going on? Bryce knew something was wrong because that was the only time Royce called him B. Bro, when will this nightmare end? I cannot go through this again. Bryce knew precisely what Royce was referring to.

Bryce listens as Royce explains the ordeal regarding Bria. His heart broke for his brother. He had seen a visible, mental, and spiritual change in Royce since his involvement with Anya. But he also saw his disappointment and pain after receiving the first results. Bryce recalls a phone call with Royce before he knew if Mia was his daughter. The excitement he heard in his voice as he planned for his future with Anya and Mia. Royce did not doubt that Anya would be a great mother to Mia. By the call's end, Royce confessed his love for Anya. The revelation at that moment for Bryce was that he was in love with Leah and could also see a future with her.

Bryce rose from his chair and headed back to his suite as he continued to talk and try to sort out this dilemma with his brother. When was the last time you spoke with Kane? Bryce asked. The communication abruptly ended shortly after the first results. Royce said. But he continued to receive photos of Mia as recently as last month. That's odd. Why would they do that if she is not yours? I am still trying to figure that out.

There is only one way to find out. You should either call Kane or Bria. Royce hesitates before answering. It would be best if I call Kane. Because I cannot promise that I would be a gentleman if I talked to Bria. Chris thinks Bria is doing this out of spite because I am in a relationship with Anya. Royce, a woman who feels scorn, is liable to do anything. Bryce stated.

Chapter 5

REALITY

Abbey exited the doors of the yoga studio. Both of her calves felt like they were on fire. It had been over two months since her last visit. Abbey thought she heard someone call her name as she walked to her vehicle. When she turned, she came face to face with a chiseled chest, abs of steel, and a smile that would light up the darkest nights.

The sweat from his drenched shirt accentuated the definition of his muscles. Abbey could not remember when she came this close and personal with the opposite sex. She refused to make eye contact with the gentleman because if she had, it would leave her questioning her decision to remain celibate.

Abbey had concluded nine months ago that she could not handle being the boss and devoting time to building a relationship with a man. A relationship that was predicated on sex only. She needed something more meaningful. And the responsibility was too much for her at the moment. She apologized to the gentleman and continued toward her car, forgetting why she had stopped.

Once inside her car, Abbey closed her eyes and took several cleansing breaths. She sat there for a few minutes, allowing herself the time to refocus. Then, redirecting her energy, Abbey picked up her phone and called Anya. Their last conversation was two weeks ago. Anya answered within seconds. Hi girlfriend. What's going on? Nothing much, just leaving the yoga studio. Did you have a good workout? I did, Abbey said. When did you get back? Late Wednesday night. Abbey loved Chicago but was ready for a change. She had been here almost seven years since she relocated from Europe.

Although Abbey loved the city's vibe, the winters were brutal. The idea of going back home to Tennessee was not an option. She needed to be somewhere warm. Abbey had considered moving back to Paris after one of her former colleagues from Berkshire Hathaway contacted her about a job opportunity there. But she chose not to because her parents were getting older, and she was their only child.

Let me rephrase that. Abbey was the only child of Beverly Winstead. Her dad, William Winstead, had two other children with his former wife, Cathryn. Her siblings would not have anything to do with her. Because they felt her mom was the cause of their parent's divorce, which was far from the truth. Anya interrupted Abbey's stroll down memory lane. I am sorry, Anya. What did you say? Can you go to Miami this weekend? If you cannot, I would understand, especially since you just returned home. Let me check and see what is on my calendar for the rest of the week, and I will get back to you. By the way, what is going on in Miami? I am looking for another property there for our satellite office. That said, I wanted to discuss partnering with you on this venture. You expressed interest in incorporating insurance concepts into your offerings a while back. Are you still considering that as an option? Yes, I am.

After my last staff meeting, I spoke with Craig about adding it to our offerings. In addition, I wanted to expand the business into other states. Plus, going somewhere that is warmer than Chicago is ideal. Anya laughed because she had previously experienced Chicago's cold winters and knew what Abbey was discussing.

Okay, let's schedule a meeting with both executive teams to discuss the legalities of this venture. That sounds great, Abbey said. I will also contact Terri to see if she can schedule the viewing for the following weekend. This should give us enough time to pull everything together. Abbey agreed and told Anya she would give her a call in the morning.

As Abbey put her car into gear to back up, she heard a loud thud. She immediately slammed on her brakes, parked the car, and looked in the rearview mirror but did not see anyone. She got out and was in shock. It was the gentlemen from earlier. He was kneeling with one hand on the bumper. Oh my God, are you all right? Do you need an ambulance? He looked up and said no. I wanted to give you this. He handed Abbey the gold Pandora bracelet, a Christmas gift from her mother. You dropped it when we collided as you were exiting the studio. Thank you, Abbey replied. You are welcome. My name is Jamerson. And you are? Abbey. It is a pleasure to run into you again. Abbey blushed and said, The pleasure is all mine. Are you sure you do not need me to call an ambulance? Yes, I am fine. Ok, thanks again. Have a good rest of your evening.

Abbey got in her car and drove off. She looked in her rearview mirror, and Jamerson was still standing there. I need a cold shower and a strong drink right about now. Abbey shook her head as she drove out of the parking lot.

The shower was exactly what Abbey needed. Now for something strong to drink. She headed downstairs to her newly renovated Selfishly Hogging Everything cave. When Abbey purchased the penthouse apartment, the space was a bedroom for the previous owner's live-in nanny. The once walk-in closet was converted into a bar, with the extra space being used as a sitting area and room to showcase her purchased African artworks and collectibles. Although Abbey was not a drinker, she loved the different shapes and colors of the wine bottles. The one thing she learned while dating her ex-boyfriend is how to select a palatable Merlot, Chardonnay, Cabernet Sauvignon, and Moscato. Abbey preferred the Pinot Grigio paired with a bowl of shrimp fettuccini, and homemade garlic bread was mouthwatering.

Unfortunately, she only had a limited inventory to select from because her ex had taken most of it when he moved out. She still had her wine coolers as a backup and a vintage 2003 bottle of Dom Perignon Champagne that she may still need to give him. Abbey grabbed the six-pack of Seagram wine coolers and headed to the kitchen, searching for the take-out menus.

She placed her delivery order with one of her favorite restaurants, Giordano's, and waited for it to arrive. The one thing Abbey can say about Chicago is that it has some top-notch eateries within walking distance from her place. The only drawback of her home is that it is minutes from Lake Michigan, and the winters are brutal. Oh, did I mention that already? Warm weather is on my horizon.

The intercom buzzed, indicating that her food had arrived. Hi Henry, evening, Ms. Winstead. Your delivery is here. Thanks, Henry. You can send them up. Henry is the doorman. Or let us say he is the Willona Woods of the building. Henry looks out for all the tenants, especially the female ones. When Abbey came to view the property with her real estate agent, Henry pulled Abbey aside to inform her about some defects not disclosed in the contract. That insightful information saved Abbey thousands of dollars. Within minutes of speaking to Henry, the delivery man was at Abbey's door with her food. As always, the food was excellent. Abbey glanced up at the clock. It was getting late. She placed the rest of her meal in the refrigerator and would take it for lunch tomorrow.

Abbey made it to work early, as usual. She entered the office, turned on the lights, and opened the blinds. She walked the short distance to her corner office and laid her monogram Buccio Tuscany Italian Leather Brown Barrister briefcase on her desk. Abbey had not slept much last night, partially because of the pain in her lower calves and her vivid dream of Jamerson.

Of all the men she dreamt about, it was of a stranger. In some regards, it was safer because she would not be running into him again anyway. Now, if she were a girl with no problem with one-night stands, he would be on that list of possibilities. Since she was not that type, dreaming about him was okay. Craig peeked into Abbey's office to let her know he was there. Good morning, Craig. Do you have a minute to talk? He did not reply. He just walked in and sat down. Your morning must not be going well because you have yet to respond. Abbey said. To answer your question, yes, my morning is going well. I was making sure. Abbey replied.

Craig Thompson was our Chief Financial Officer and was a genius at what he did. Abbey was introduced to Craig while completing an internship with the World Bank Group. Several top-notch financial institutions had recruited

Craig right out of school. He could have accepted any of their offers but settled with Abbey's small up-and-coming firm. Everyone in the office knew Craig was an overachiever, which is a plus, especially when managing money. Abbey and Craig's relationship is unorthodox. He is an introvert with little to no social skills. It took Abbey three years to convince him that there were other colors in the crayon box outside: black, brown, and white. He occasionally wears tan or red when feeling dangerous, which is rare. Craig, I wanted to discuss a business venture involving Anya McMichael's company and ours.

I mentioned adding more offerings to our portfolio at our last staff meeting. Something in the healthcare industry is ideal. What are your thoughts? Well, anything in that industry is a winner. Healthcare is going nowhere because someone will always need medical treatment. However, doing business with a friend is like doing business with family. I know how highly you speak about Anya. I would not want your relationship to be ruined because of business. Craig had a valid point. Abbey and Anya had previously partnered on business collaborations, but not to this magnitude. Craig said I am not opposed to discussing potential business opportunities with Anya's team. But you should be clear about how this business arrangement will work first.

Chapter 6

UNEASY

The ride to work seemed longer for Leah than usual. Then, it dawned on her that Bryce had been driving her to work for the last month. When she woke up this morning, she was very emotional. Leah could not understand why. Bryce had been away for business before. But something in her gut told her this trip was different.

The last year with Bryce has been a fairytale. Leah had grown and evolved as a person and certainly as a woman. Suppose someone told her she would be in a relationship and living with a man a year ago. She would have laughed at them. But Leah still found herself pinching herself to ensure she was not dreaming. They are still learning about one another. And have disagreements like any other couple.

After their first date, the driver brought them back to her place. Leah invited Bryce to stay because he still needed to make accommodations for lodging. Although he looked and smelled good, Leah had to remember what her Granny said, "Your Body Is Your Temple, And It is Sacred. Be Wise As To Whom You Allow To Enter It." Even though they had an excellent evening, he was still not getting the cookie. In this instance, Leah needed to think like a man and act like a woman. Thanks, Uncle Steve!

That night, Leah and Bryce made it official. They were in an exclusive relationship. They talked the rest of the night, and Bryce slept in her guest room for the next week until he flew home. Ladies, it was Bryce's idea not to become intimate until they both were ready. Then, he suggested that they go to couples therapy. Not because we were having problems but because he wanted to be in a healthy and stable relationship from the beginning.

In one of their sessions, the therapist asked them to define intimacy. We both gave what we thought intimacy meant. However, our definition was far from its true meaning. The therapist pointed out that we did not mention the word desire. Both Bryce and I looked perplexed.

The therapist explained that we must desire intimacy enough to make the time to gain the ability to be transparent and open. Be vulnerable and willing to endure temporary pain or setbacks along the way. Leah had never considered the importance of desire in any of her romantic or platonic relationships. The way the therapist explained it with passion and conviction resonated in her spirit. Leah could see that Bryce felt it, too. Ultimately, it is a choice to desire your mate. Leah knows what she felt for Bryce was desire and love. These are the times she wished she had her mother.

Leah's mind wandered back to when her mom was pregnant with her younger sister. She began acting out in school, which was not like her. The principal had called Leah to the office because she had punched Terrell Jefferson in the stomach. After all, he said that all momma was good for was having babies. He is lucky that Leah was the one who punched him, not one of my older brothers.

When I got to the office, Momma was there. I was expecting my dad. But boy, I was glad he was not there. Mr. Steele was our principal and was meaner than a bear awakened during hibernation season. I know he would have suspended me from school. For some reason, his demeanor was much softer whenever he saw Momma.

Mr. Steele and Momma reprimanded me for my actions and gave me a choice to either go home and think about what I did or have Mr. Steele suspend me and call Dad. Of course, I chose the first option.

Mr. Steele allowed me to leave with Momma. The ride home was quiet. Momma had not said anything since we left the school. Leah knew that her mother was disappointed with her. As they pulled into the house's front yard, Momma looked at me and said, "Leah, never allow anyone to make you so mad that you forget who you are and how you were raised. "I love every child that I have carried and birth. And it is no one's business how many your father and I chose to have. I will not tell your father about this incident, but you will have additional chores added to your list for the next month. And Leah, I don't condone violence, but I bet you that Terrell Jefferson will think twice about saying something about your Momma. We laughed, got out of the car, and entered the house.

Later that evening, after completing the kitchen chores, Leah decided to walk to the creek. She sat on the edge of the fishing pier and took her shoes off. The cool water on her feet was like heaven on earth. She swooped up a handful of water and splashed it on her face and the back of her neck. Then, she took out her journal and started to write down today's events. The only thing Leah wrote was HORRIBLE DAY EVER!

Leah spotted her parents in the backyard when she returned to the house. Dad pushed Mom onto the swing hanging from the giant oak tree. You would think that they were newlyweds. The way Momma laughed was filled with giddiness. Dad gently touched Momma's back to push her into the breeze. Their love was magical. Leah did not doubt that her parents desired one another. But how she wished that she could have had the chance to ask her.

Leah pulled her cell phone from her purse and dialed Bryce's number but stopped when she remembered the time difference. So she texted him: LEAH- Good morning, darling. Have a wonderful day. You owe me big time when you return home.

Leah did not know why she felt compelled to want to see Bryce. But something subconsciously told her she did. She pulled her car into the drive-thru line at Steak & Shake. She needed to take her mind off of Bryce. Leah ordered two breakfast burritos, hash browns with onions and cheese, a large Sprite, and mild picante sauce on the side.

Was I hungry, or was it my nerves? To be honest, it was both. Leah thought. She pulled the car into an open space and began eating. The meal was just what she needed. Leah had just placed the empty containers in the bag when her phone rang.

Hey Love. I see that I am not the only one thinking about someone. Leah was smiling from ear to ear. What are you doing up? I could not sleep. And then I got this text from this beautiful lady. So, she tells me that I owe her big time when I return home. Oh, did she? Yes, she did. So, have you thought about what she might want? I have some thoughts.

When I get home, I have something special for that beautiful lady. Leah said, sound as if you are smitten with this woman. Yes, more than I think she knows, Bryce replied. Well, that lady is truly blessed to have such a wonderful man like yourself in her life. And I know in her heart she is smitten with you, too.

Leah arrived at work in a better frame of mind after talking with Bryce. She opened the door to her office, and immediately, the room began to spin out of nowhere, followed by nausea and lower abdominal pain. Leah immediately grabbed the corner of the desk to steady her unbalanced gait and eased herself into the chair.

She laid her head on the teakwood desk, praying that the coolness would wash away the heat she was now feeling. Panic soon began to settle as Leah was the only one in the suite. The others would not be in for another hour. Leah reached for her purse in search of her cell phone but could not find it. Finally, she picked up the receiver on the desk phone and pressed one on the keypad. The call went to Anya's cellphone. Before Leah could say anything, she passed out.

Chapter 7

CARVING OUT TIME

Sal was up early reviewing the latest financial report that his assistant had emailed him last night. His thoughts went back to when he received the unexpected call from Lourdes two days ago; he had no idea she would be here in Arizona. Sal looked up from the papers on the desk as the door from the bathroom opened.

Good morning. How did you sleep? Like a baby. The bartender from last night walked toward Sal, placing her hand on his bare chest. I enjoyed our time together last night. It was lovely. She gathered her clothing from the floor, indicating that she needed to go. I hope you enjoy the rest of your time here in Arizona, and maybe I will see you again. You will, Sal said.

Salvatore De La Cruz was no stranger to hard work. As a young boy, it was instilled in him that a closed mouth doesn't get fed. Sal began working alongside his grandparents at age eight at their family's Colorado hacienda during the summer. He remembers waking up at four in the morning to prepare the feed for the livestock, checking the crops for insects and beetles, and collecting fresh eggs and milk for breakfast. His Abuela would have already gathered the other items in the kitchen as she prepared the morning chow for the ranch hands.

The Santos Ranchero employed seventy-five employees responsible for over one hundred acres of land in the Colorado Plains Region, bordering the Rocky Mountains foothills West of Kansas. Sal's grandfather Esposito Santos began cultivating the land in nineteen sixty-nine at thirty-one with his grandmother Cecilia and brother Diego.

They started with a small herd of cattle and sheep. In the last fifty-four years, they have amassed more acreage, which is now used to harvest corn, wheat, barley, peaches, and apples. Ranch life may appear to the outside world as slow-paced and relaxing, but it is hectic and hard work. And Sal experienced that firsthand.

Sal, his brother, and cousins came to the ranch each summer primarily to spend time with their grandparents but mostly to give their parents a break. Lou was one of those cousins who lived at the ranchero. Her father was my Uncle Eddie. Uncle Eddie was named after our grandfather but preferred to be called Eddie out of respect for his father.

Lourdes Esmeralda Santos-Vicente was my uncle Eddie's daughter and eldest. Uncle Eddie spared no expense when it came to Lou, which caused a wedge between her brothers and her parents. The bickering between Uncle Eddie and Aunt Risa ultimately caused them to divorce.

The divorce affected my cousins and caused a rift between my mom and Uncle Eddie. Hence, the reason why I grew up in Florida. Mom had chosen to side with my Aunt Risa when she put Lou out of the house when she was caught having sex with her now ex-husband in their bedroom. This was after she was kicked out of public and private school, had numerous traffic tickets, and was charged with underage drinking DUI, and she did not want to work. Uncle Eddie felt Mom should have taken his side because he was her brother.

When Sal received Lou's call, it had been five years. That is when he saw her last at their Uncle Diego's funeral. She was still estranged from her siblings and parents. Uncle Eddie had remarried, and she did not get along with the new wife because she had given birth to her little sister, Sasha. Sal was unable to comprehend Lou's reasoning regarding this matter. After all, Lou was an adult while Sasha was still a child.

After Bryce left the dinner table last night, Sal had a one-on-one conversation with her and her reason for being in Arizona. Lou explained that once her relationship with her family had fallen apart and her husband left her, she realized she had no one, and that was because of her own doing. So she relocated to Santa Fe, New Mexico, to start fresh. Lou knew that if she did not get control of her life, everything she touched or was involved with would be destroyed.

While in Santa Fe, she met her mentor and now business partner. She refocused her life on the things that brought her joy. But she knew that something was missing. As a child, Lou always felt like she did not belong. She would always question her parents why she did not look like anyone in the family. The answer she got was always the same. You look like your maternal great-grandmother. But no one could ever provide her with a picture of her.

UNMASK

Finally, five years after Uncle Diego's funeral, Lou received a letter from him. Sal looked at Lou as if she had lost her mind. Lou handed the letter to Sal.

Lula Belle,

If you are receiving this letter, I am no longer here. I have struggled over the years as I watched you grow up, not knowing why you were different from all the others. It has been said in many cultures that knowing where you come from is the basis of your identity. It is time you hear the truth.

June 25, 1982, was the day I first laid eyes on your mother. She had come to the ranch seeking employment as a ranch hand. During that time, it was rare for women to want to work in the field doing such manual labor. We all looked at her and laughed. Your mother was very petite, short in stature, and weighed less than a three-string square bale of hay. But she quickly made us look like fools. She could handle herself like any man on the crew, maybe even better.

One evening after chow, she was outside the barn brushing down one of the horses, and I walked over and struck up a conversation with her. I did all of the talking. She just listened. This went on for several weeks. I could not figure out why she would not talk to me. Your Abuela saw my frustration and pointed out that maybe she was shy and did not know what to say.

About a month later, I was mending one of the fences just north of the ranchero when she approached me and began talking. Our talks were about life on the ranch. The conversation went silent whenever I addressed her family and where she was from. It did not take long to realize that the topic of the family was off-limits. I would let her talk about that when she was ready.

We soon made the north pasture our getaway. We would talk for hours about really nothing. Many times, we would sit in silence. We were out in the pasture one evening when a severe thunderstorm was approaching, and we had to return the herd to the stables. The winds picked up, and clouds rolled in, causing the skies to go black as the night. We got the pack back to the stables safely. But the thunder was relentless, casting strikes that could be heard about ten miles away. The fear in your mother's eyes when the bolt of the lighting lit up the entire cloud base, causing her to run in my arms, let me know she was not as hard as she pretended to be.

The following weekend was the annual Ranchero Harvest Festival. The formal gathering celebrated the contribution of Latinos to agriculture. Your mother was quiet that entire week, and I assumed she was embarrassed because of the storm incident. The night of the festival, I had not seen her. Not until she entered the room in a pale blue formal gown accentuating her curves. The ones hidden by the baggy denim trousers and oversized shirt she wore every day. Her light brown hair hung to the middle of her back. And the subdued makeup was natural, showcasing her beautiful brown eyes. Your Abuela waved her over to sit at her table. I could not take my eyes off her the entire night.

Finally, the night was about to end, and the announcer advised the last call for drinks and dancing. I took a big gulp of liquid courage and asked her to dance. We danced long after the music had stopped and the people had begun leaving. That night is stamped in my heart and memory for eternity. Three months later, your mother received a call that caused her to revert to being withdrawn. Shortly afterward, she left, and we did not hear from her again. It was in October of the following year. I received a call from a social worker advising that I had a six-month-old daughter and that if I did not want you to go into the foster care system, I needed to come and get you immediately, or my parental rights would be terminated. I was stunned because your mother and I were never intimate. I knew I needed to act quickly. I boarded the plane to Alberta, Canada, and brought you home.

Sal was speechless as Lou handed him numerous handwritten letters from Uncle Diego. His question for Lou was why Uncle Eddie and Aunt Risa assumed the role of your parents. Lou indicated Aunt Risa had suffered a miscarriage just before Uncle Diego came back with her, and to ease the pain of the loss, she found comfort in carrying for her. Lou said. Sal, I am grateful for the life that Papi and Mami gave me, but I deserve to know whose blood runs in my veins.

Lou handed Sal a picture. Uncle Diego said this picture was taken on the night of the formal. It was as if Sal was staring at an image of Lou, only a younger version. Uncle Diego believes that my mom was forced into an arranged marriage or was in an abusive one when she ended up at the ranch. The birth certificate listed:

Sex: Female

Name: Ava Marie Redmon   Type of Birth: Single

Place of Birth: Toronto General Hospital

City: Toronto, Ontario, Canada

DOB: May 18, 1983

CALENTHIA YVETTE MILLER

Mother: Selena Marie Redmon

Age: 24

DOB: May 16, 1959

Marital Status: Single

Place of Birth: Toronto, Ontario, Canada

Race: Black/Hispanic

Father: Unknown

Age: 25

DOB: April 6, 1958

Marital Status: Unknown

Place of Birth: Africa

Race: Caucasian

Lou begins to cry as she tries to speak. My emotions have been all over the place. I received my birth certificate and this letter two weeks ago. Sal, why was I not good enough to keep? Am I a reminder of her abusive husband? Who am I? The person I thought I was doesn't exist. Did she risk her life to save mine? What is her story?

Sal could not imagine the turmoil that Lou was experiencing. His heart ached for her and wished he could take the pain she felt away. Sal asked, have you talked to your parents? No. I don't know what to say. And I have no clue what to do. Lou looked exhausted after their talk. Sal walked Lou to her room and returned to the bar for a nightcap. He knew he needed to do something to help his cousin. He had written down Lou's birth mother's information and would pass it on to his lawyer in the morning.

Sal had finished reviewing the financial reports and took an extra-long shower, hoping to wash away the events of last night. Then, as promised, he called his lawyer and gave her the information on Lourdes's mother. In addition, he provided information on her potential father. His lawyer advised that finding Lou's father would be like searching for a needle in a haystack. He then called Bryce and Lou to remind them about the inspection scheduled for that afternoon and headed out the door.

Chapter 8

LIMITLESS POSSIBILITIES

Marisa had arrived at the television station a few hours early. She still needed to gather additional information on a story airing at noon. As she exited the break room, her assignment editor, Carl, approached her about covering a story on British Prime Minister Boris Johnson. Marisa was on cloud nine and could not believe her ears. Since returning to the newsroom earlier this year, she has worked hard to prove herself. And it is finally paying off.

Nevertheless, she immediately agreed to take the assignment. Carl asked her to meet him in his office to discuss the job details. Instantly, Marisa called Sebastián first to tell him her news. He was just as happy as she was. He knew that journalism was her passion. But there was a time when Marisa would have questioned calling Sebastián.

A few weeks after returning from their family trip to the mountains last year, Marisa had an epiphany about her relationship with Sebastián and herself. That epiphany was triggered by her candid conversation with him regarding Ocean.

When Marisa first met Sebastián, she knew their connection was genuine. He did not have an ulterior motive. Like most of the guys she met during her college years. Sebastian saw her for her brains and not her beauty. She remembers their first conversation in his dorm room after the National Black Student Union meeting.

He asked what I was majoring in. I responded to journalism. And he then asked what I would do if war broke out. I answered without hesitation go where the story took me. His reasons for asking that question never dawned on her until last year.

Several things struck a chord during that candid and heartfelt conversation she had with Sebastián. And one of those things was that he never asked for anything in return. Not even love or respect. The first time Marisa heard Sebastián say he loved her was last year when they spoke on the phone regarding the conversation Ocean overheard Marisa having with her girlfriend.

But, even then, he did not expect anything in return. Marisa realized that Sebastián only saw her as the pure, unfiltered version. He needed to know that when war broke out, Marisa would not hesitate to go where the story was, where he and Ocean were. But subconsciously, Marisa was selfish and had forgotten that Sebastián had put his life on hold for her to travel the globe covering stories with her and then move across the country because he loved her and their unborn child. Sebastián may not have said he loved her, but he showed it countless times in his actions.

It has taken several months to return to a place where they are good. However, Marisa would not trade this experience for anything in the world. It has taught her to never take people for granted and to speak up and work purposefully in your truth because you are the only one who can tell your story.

Once Ocean and Marisa moved into the farmhouse with Sebastián, they tried to rekindle their relationship but quickly realized that too much time had passed, and they had changed as people. And Marisa knew his heart belonged to another. And she had her eye on someone else. The connection that she has with this person is organic. They have endless conversations about everything and laugh about the silliest things. The crazy thing about this is that Sebastián noticed the connection before Marisa did. Their relationship is a thousand times better, and Marisa could not be happier. Nor could Ocean. Marisa was torn about going on the assignment to London, especially when she found out that it would be taking place when Ocean would be receiving her awards. It had taken some time for her relationship with Ocean to mend as well, and she could not jeopardize the progress that they had made. So once she had spoken with Sebastián, she FaceTime Ocean. She found she could see her genuine reaction in real-time when doing this. Ocean answered on the first ring.

I swear that kid sleeps with that device in her hand.

Good morning. Are you up and getting ready for school? I am sorry! I just remembered that I had left a few hours early for work. I wanted to talk with you about something. Ok, Ocean said as she repositioned herself in bed. I have been offered to cover a story in London. But it is the same time as your award ceremony. I had no idea when I accepted the job. So, I will go back and decline. Ocean just looked at her and did not say anything.

Finally, when Marisa finished rambling, Ocean said, "Mom, I know how hard you have worked since returning to the news station. This is a great opportunity, and you may not get another one. So please do it. Plus, you don't need my permission to go after your dream. You have supported me all of my life. Now it is time that I support you. I am proud of you, Mom." Marisa undoubtedly had no words. She had to look away from the camera as she began to cry. This was indeed Sebastián's child. Like he, she had a heart of gold and thought of others before themselves. Two days before the ceremony, Sebastián and Ocean drove Marisa to the airport. She met her new friend there, who agreed to accompany her on her first international trip in fifteen years. Marisa is truly blessed to have such a great support system in place.

Chapter 9

YOUR MOVE

Royce had worked longer than usual. Since he and Anya moved in together, Royce had made it a habit that he would be home by six each night. He glanced down at the letter he had received from Chris a few days ago. Things had been going so well between him and Anya this last year. How was he going to tell her about this?

They planned to relocate to Miami in a few months, and Royce booked a memorable getaway for them in a few weeks. Royce had tried to connect with Kane but was unsuccessful. He knew that if he did not speak with him soon, he would be forced to call Bria, something he dreaded doing.

Stephen stopped in before leaving and asked if he needed anything before leaving for the night. Bryce indicated no. Stephen reminded Royce about his deposition in the morning at eight and the executive leadership meeting at eleven before leaving.

Royce had turned off his computer and placed the case files in his briefcase. When he looked up, Anya was standing at the door. I thought you might be hungry and handed Bryce what he needed—a Philly steak and cheese with mushrooms, onions, and a Dr. Pepper. Royce smiled. I called you earlier and figured you were working late when you had not arrived home. Thanks, baby. I am sorry today has been a busy day. Anya placed her manicured finger on Royce's lips. Shh, it's ok. I understand. In the back of Bryce's mind, he prayed she would understand what he was about to tell her regarding the paternity testing. Baby, sit down and eat.

Anya watched as Royce ate the last of his sandwich. Are you ready for dessert? Anya asked. I am stuffed. Are you sure? Royce pushed away from the desk and placed the bag in the trash, and when he turned back toward Anya, she was sitting on the couch with nothing on. Royce was mesmerized by the way the moonlight framed her body. And how her hair hung covering her breast. Royce slowly walked toward Anya. He was taking in how beautiful she looked. Anya stood, took Royce's hand, and guided him onto the couch. She began removing his suit jacket, then his shirt. Finally, she whispered in his right ear:" Let me take care of you tonight."

Anya placed soft kisses along his neck, collarbone, and full lips. Royce's body began to react as she made trails of kisses to his navel. Next, Anya removed his socks and shoes and unbuckled his slacks. Looking back up at Royce, Anya eased his pants off. She was causing Royce to grow tense as she blew cool air on his jewels and slowly mounted him. A primal growl erupted from Royce's throat, sending her mind into a frenzy. Anya rode Royce like the waves in Percy Priest Lake.

Royce pulled her mouth toward his, passionately kissing her as his tongue mated with hers. Anya opened her legs wider as Royce grew inside her, causing Anya's walls to expand. Anya threw her head back as Royce released her swollen lips and grasped her entire breast in his mouth, sucking like a newborn baby learning how to nurse. He softly bit her nipple, causing a slight sting that made Anya's muscles tighten. Her pace picked up as her hips swayed rhythmically with Royce. Royce's growls became louder.

Finally, he lifted Anya and laid her back on the couch. She locked her legs around his muscular back and placed her arms around his neck. Royce could feel Anya's walls fall, and he was precisely where he needed to be. They stared into each other's eyes as their waves collided, causing them to become one. They lay there in beautiful bliss in the moonlight. They made love several more times before heading home. Royce knew tonight would not be the night he told Anya about the paternity test. But he knew he had to. They had vowed never to keep any secrets between them. He just needed the right time to tell her.

Once in the house, their sexual escapade continued. Royce wanted her even more. He could not get enough of her. Anya felt free to explore every inch of Royce's body. There was no area untouched. Their lovemaking ended just where it began, wrapped in one another arms on the rooftop under the moonlight. Royce looked down at Anya as she slept peacefully. He prayed she would remain by his side once he told her about this new paternity test. He could hear Mr. Overton say, "Whatever you are going through, this too shall pass. Trust in the process; your time to love again is coming." He traced the outline of Anya's lips with the tip of his finger. Bryce knew his time was now with Anya. He loved her and only her. NO SECRETS!

Chapter 10

MEETING IN THE LADY'S ROOM

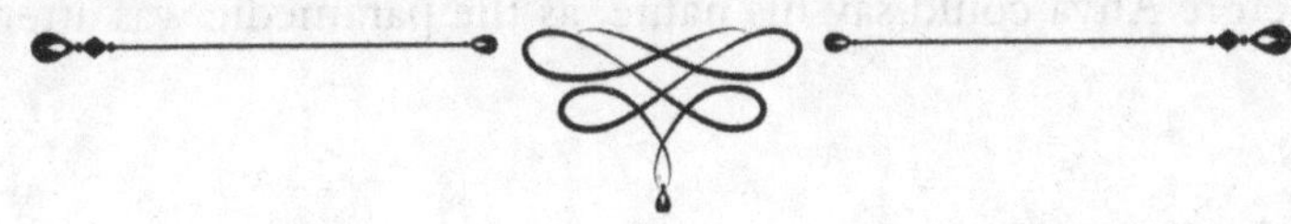

Anya had stopped by the coffee shop before heading into the office. She needed some caffeine to replenish the energy and the calories she had burnt this morning with Royce. So she left him in bed this morning. Checkmate Mission Accomplished!

Just as Anya entered the elevator, her cell phone rang, but she lost connection when the doors closed. When Anya made it to her floor, she had a missed call from Leah's extension. As expected, she was here early, even on the weekend. She unlocked the doors and called out her name. No response. Anya headed to the ladies' room, and Leah was not there. She made her way to the boardroom, and still no Leah. She called her cellphone, and still no answer. Anya proceeded down the hall to her office and noticed the light was on in Leah's office. She called her cell phone and could hear it ringing. She cautiously walked toward her office and saw Leah's legs from behind the desk. She immediately rounded the desk and went to her. Anya checked her pulse, ensured she was breathing, and immediately called for an ambulance. After speaking with the 911 operator, she called Royce, and he, in return, called Bryce. Finally, Anya called Sebastián because she knew he could hear the radio traffic and did not want him to become alarmed.

Good morning. Is everything OK? Sebastián ask. Yes. I wanted to let you know that I had to call an ambulance to the office just in case you were near your radio or scanner. I found Leah in her office unresponsive, and we were on the way to the hospital. It's like Déjà vu. The only difference is that Royce came in before Anya could say his name, as the paramedic was attending to Leah.

Sebastián could hear a male voice and automatically put two and two together and figured it out. There was an awkward silence between them, so Sebastián said," I would let you go, and thanks for calling me." He hung up before Anya could say anything further.

Leah had regained consciousness as she was being loaded into the ambulance. Leah asked the paramedic what had happened. Ms. Bernard, your friend, found you unresponsive on the floor in your office. Can you tell me what happened? I began to feel dizzy and nauseous. Have you been experiencing COVID-like symptoms, such as runny nose, fever, nausea, headache, diarrhea, or vomiting? Yes, I have experienced nausea and vomiting. Have you been tested for COVID-19 in the last ten days or potentially been exposed to anyone with COVID-19? Leah answered no; I haven't been tested and don't believe so. Do you think you could be pregnant, and when was her last menstrual period? Leah could give a sure answer to that question because she had not missed her cycle, and it was due to come on; OH, HOCKEY

STICK! Six days ago.

Royce helped Anya into the ambulance and told her he would meet her at the hospital. Once the paramedic stabilized Leah, Anya sat beside her, held her hand, and reassured her that everything would be okay. Bryce called just before they made it to the hospital. By this time, Leah was crying hysterically. Anya had to take the phone from Leah because her oxygen level was dropping. Anya talked with Bryce; he said he was going to the airport and would be home by two today. Anya let Leah know, which significantly improved her oxygen level. They immediately took Leah to a room once they arrived at the hospital. Anya went to the waiting area and waited on Royce. The attendant finally came out and spoke with them after three hours. The doctor advised that they would test Leah for COVID and flu and get a pregnancy test. They could see Leah once she was confirmed negative for COVID and the flu. Royce had to leave to pick Bryce up from the airport. Anya could talk with Leah because she still had her cell phone.

It was another hour before the results came back that Leah was positive for COVID-19, negative for flu, and there was a trace of HCG in her urine sample, which means she was also pregnant. So, the doctor said she would like to confirm the pregnancy through a blood draw. Anya could hear in Leah's voice the fear. Oh, how she wished she could be there to hug her. Anya opted to FaceTime since she could not go into the room.

How do I tell Bryce that we are pregnant? Anya said let's wait to confirm the pregnancy, and then you can tell him. Anya, we have only been together a year. We barely know one another. I understand your concern. Leah, do you love Bryce? Yes, with all of my heart. Do you see a future with him? Yes. Then, the hard part is over. Leah laughed and began to cough uncontrollably. Then suddenly the monitors on the machine started to alarm. Leah dropped the phone, and a swarm of people was in the room within seconds.

Anya could see that Leah's eyes had rolled back into her head, and her beautiful caramel tone had turned the color of clay. She could hear over the hospital intercom Code Blue Emergency Response Team Emergency Room Bed Nine. The announcement alerted me three more times before it ended. Anya immediately began to pray for restoration from the crown of Leah's head to the soles of her feet. A peace came over Anya as she asked God to restore harmony and wholeness to her womb.

The receptionist from the front desk called out Anya's name. As to say, your prayers have been granted. Ms. McMichael, the attendant, would like to meet with you in the family room. Anya did not become fearful because she did not doubt the power of God. The attendant informed Anya that Leah had to be placed on a ventilator because she had COVID-related pneumonia. She advised that this would only be temporary if Leah responded well to the antibiotics. Anya called Royce and filled him in on everything. She called Leah's father and had Stacie make flight arrangements for him and Leah's siblings. In addition, they had the rooms at the Air BNB prepared for them when they arrived.

Chapter 11

THINGS ARE NOT WHAT THEY APPEAR

Chris was still confused by what he had witnessed a few days ago. There were two of them. Ms. Dominique Sanchez has a twin sister who happens to be the receptionist. But Chris is still trying to figure out why; when he called the office for the second time, did Dominique answer? Chris needed to get a bit more information on the Sanchez sisters. In his gut, there is more than what it appears to be.

The chiming of the ringer indicated that he had made it to his floor. Pulling out the rack card he had taken from the desk at Ms. Sanchez's office last week. Her profile indicated that she volunteered for this not-for-profit organization in her spare time. Canvas of Thoughts was a literacy program that provided additional resources such as housing and clothing for domestic abuse survivors. The owner and CEO, Misha Saunders, agreed to talk with Chris about the program.

Many programs such as this are born out of our experiences, which is true in Ms. Saunders's case. Misha's mother was in an abusive relationship with her now-deceased father. The abuse for her was generational because she had witnessed it with her mother, grandmother, and older sister. She found refuge in reading books, which her mother and grandmother struggled with. Misha met Dominique and Darcy at a shelter when she was nine. Dominique's mother had fled Cuba after her father was killed. Neither Dominique, Darcy, nor their mother spoke, read, or wrote English. Misha taught Dominique, and this is how their friendship began. Misha advised that Dominique was and continues to be a big supporter of the program. Chris wrapped up his conversation with Misha and thanked her for her time.

Chris still felt he was overlooking something. He headed into the office to pull the case file and transcripts from Lucas's trial; maybe he would find it there. Still no luck. He asked Loren, his administrative and legal assistant, to review the file. Chris's cell phone rang as he pulled into his assigned parking space at his condo. He answered without looking at the caller's identification. Hello, Mr. Calloway. This is Dominique Sanchez. My apologies for not returning your call sooner. As an attorney, you know we are always swamped. Good day, Ms. Sanchez. Thanks for returning my call. No problem; how can I help you? I had the opportunity to confer with my client, Mr. Blackmon, and we are questioning the validity of Mr. White's claims. Secondly, your correspondence advised that there was evidence of tampering with the previous sample. Ms. Sanchez, that is a bold allegation. This not only places reasonable doubt in the operation of the Coventry Hospital outpatient lab and its collection process, which is very interesting as my client had his sample collected at a private diagnostic site. It could also lead to many others questioning their results, especially the paternity testing if that allegation is made public.

In addition, are there supporting medical records showing a vasectomy was performed, and do you have a semen analysis to confirm that Mr. White cannot conceive a child? Lastly, has the other alleged father been contacted as well?

There was a long pause before Ms. Sanchez replied. Mr. Calloway, I understand that you and your client have reservations regarding the paternity test and Mr. White's timing. But I assure you his claim is legitimate. The results regarding my client's fertility will be sent to you by the end of the week. And the other alleged fathers have been contacted.

Chris replayed Ms. Sanchez's last statement, "Contact with the other FATHERS." Who are the other fathers besides Nate and Lucas? How many partners did Bria have during the time of conception? He needed to talk with Royce as soon as possible. Are there any other questions I can answer for you, Mr. Calloway?

No. But Mr. Blackmon has also opted to have the paternity test done at a private outpatient diagnostic clinic again. I will inform you of that date and time. That would be great. Ms. Sanchez advised. Please don't hesitate to reach out if you have additional questions or concerns.

Chris immediately called Royce and informed him of his conversation with Ms. Sanchez. Chris still felt that something did not add up with her. When he returns to the office, he will follow up with Loren to see if she has found anything in the case file.

Chris unlocked the door to his condo. He stood at the threshold and reflected on how far he had come from the days of eating Ramen noodles in his dorm room, working several jobs, and picking up every extra hour to put himself through law school. He definitely could not take all of the credit for his success.

His mother had raised him and his brother in a loving and nurturing home. She did not play when it came to hard work and school. Mom always said, "Once you have obtained knowledge, no one can take it from you." Chris knows that his hard work is paying off. He works for one of the most affluent law firms in the country, debt-free, healthy, and living his best life. What more could he ask for?

Chapter 12

I CAN NOT

When Royce called Bryce, he had just finished eating breakfast and was leaving to meet Sal and Lou in the hotel lobby. Good morning. Hey bro, are you able to talk? Yes. Leah had to be rushed to the hospital. Anya found her unresponsive at the office this morning. Before Royce could finish his sentence, he said I am on my way and hung up.

Bryce called the airline and made the first available reservation. He then called Anya, and they were still enroute to the hospital. Bryce could hear the medics asking Leah questions but could not determine her answers. Finally, he heard Anya tell her that he was on the phone.

Hi, beautiful lady. Don't talk; listen. I need you to relax and breathe. I am on my way, and I love you and owe you something. Leah laughed, and she gave the phone back to Anya. Bryce relayed his travel itinerary to Anya and asked that she take care of Leah until he arrived.

He stopped, took a deep cleansing breath, and let it out slowly. Bryce thought about the conversation with the couple's therapist about desiring our mate, his mother's long sleepless nights at the bedside when his father was in the hospital, his last talk with Skylar, and the devastation Royce felt after losing her. He could not lose Leah. They had so much more to do and see. Leah was the first woman he could and wanted to spend the rest of his life with. Tears began forming in his eyes as he returned to his room. Just as he turned the corner, he ran into Lou.

Bryce apologized; I was preoccupied. Are you ok? I will be Bryce said. Can you tell Sal I had a family emergency and need to leave? I will give him a call once I can. Lou nodded her head. Bryce packed his belongings and called the front to ensure he could catch the next shuttle to the airport.

Bryce called Anya, and his call went to voicemail. He then called Royce and told him when his flight would arrive. Next, he called his mom. He knew Ella would know what to do and say. Bryce filled her in with what he knew. Son, there is power in prayer. You need to pray. Bryce said Mom, "What if you don't know how to do that." Speak from your heart, son. Nothing that you say to God is a surprise. He can hear and feel you. Be purposeful in your prayers. And remember, your relationship with God is unique, and He places no judgment on you or me. He wants us to come to Him for His guidance and love.

Bryce was nervous but began:
I am trying to figure out what to say or where to begin. But Momma said to

speak from my heart. It has been a long time since I talked with you. I don't even deserve to ask you for anything. But, God, I have never felt anything like this for any woman. Leah is different. I would give my life for her. This may be selfish, but I am not ready to give her up. Please watch and take care of her until I arrive home. I promise to care for and cherish her as you do for all of your children. Thank you for all the blessings seen and unseen.

Amen

Bryce felt a sense of peace after he had prayed. He was so thankful because, at this very moment, he knew he was no longer alone. The phone rang in the room; the desk clerk said the shuttle would arrive in ten minutes. The ride to the airport seemed to take forever. All Bryce wanted was to see Leah. He was unsure if he was strong enough to weather that storm should anything happen to her before he got there.

The plane had reached Dallas, and Bryce was waiting on his connecting flight to Tennessee. He immediately called Anya for any updates, but it went to voicemail. He then dialed Royce's number, and he did not answer either. Just as he was about to call Anya again, Sal called. He extended his prayers to Bryce and advised him to contact him when things were stable.

Bryce called several times before he reached Royce, who reported they were still waiting for the attendant to speak with them regarding Leah's condition. Royce reassured Bryce that he and Anya would keep him abreast of everything. Bryce thanked Royce and, in a melancholy voice, said," I could not lose her. Leah is my world." Royce replied I know she is, bro. We are holding it down here until you arrive. Bryce ended their call and prepared to board the plane home to Leah. Once in the air, Bryce said another silent prayer before he closed his eyes.

Chapter 13

SHARED RESPONSIBILITIES

Abbey had tried unsuccessfully to reach Anya after a missed call from her on Saturday morning. Their teams were due to meet virtually at ten that Monday. Her recent conversation with Craig still played in her head. Abbey knew a lot was at stake, but she felt confident that she and Anya were mature enough to separate their business relationship from their own. She finally connected with Anya and was told she had found Leah passed out on Saturday on the floor in her office. Abbey was shocked after Anya provided her with the details of Leah's condition. What struck Abbey was that Leah was the same age as she was. In their conversation, Anya expressed the importance of vaccinating and taking all the necessary precautions to keep ourselves and those around us safe.

Abbey had received her COVID booster just before she left for her last business trip. Most of the staff had been vaccinated, and the ones who chose not could work remotely until further notice. Once Abbey had finished conversing with Anya, she immediately called her parents to confirm their vaccination status.

Although Abbey's parents were getting older, they were in good health. However, her dad had a health scare about two years ago when his prostate screening showed abnormal. But because of regular visits to the doctor, they were able to detect the cancer early. Abbey's father confirmed that he and her mother had already received their COVID-19 and flu vaccines.

After speaking with her parents, Abbey decided to head to her nine o'clock yoga class. Her calves have felt much better since the last workout. So she pulled her gym bag from the backseat of the car and headed in. Unfortunately, the gym was rather busy on a Sunday. Abbey glanced at the posted schedule, and her yoga class had been canceled. And the next one was not until next week. So she opted to stay and swim a few laps in the Olympic-sized pool to kill time before meeting her parents for lunch. Beverly Winstead had called late Thursday night to inform Abbey that she and her dad would be in Chicago for the annual Prostate Prevention Conference that weekend.

Abbey quickly changed into her swimsuit and headed to the pool. When Abbey opened the glass doors, she was surprised that no one was there. She removed the towel wrapped around her waist and placed it and her cell phone on the chair steps from the pool. She eased her body into the cool water, and instantly, any problem she had faded away. Abbey submerged her head underneath, allowing her body and mind to relax as the tranquility of the blue water surrounded her. Her strokes were precise as she glided down the length of the pool. Abbey had finished the last fifty meters of her lap, stepped out of the pool, and retrieved the towel left on the chair.

UNMASK

The door opened, causing a breeze to enter the space as she wiped the excess water from her face and body. Abbey looked up, and it was Jamerson. A mirage of images ran through her mind. Not only had she dreamt of him every night since she damn near ran him over. However, the visions of him in her dream did not compare to what he looked like in person.

Good morning. So, we meet again. Abbey tried not to stare, but she could not help herself. This man looked as if he had just stepped off the cover of the GQ magazine. His oversized silhouette cast a temporary darkness as he approached Abbey. Jamerson's broad shoulders could hold two small books on them. The clef in his chin was sexy as it complimented his beautiful smile. Abbey lowered her eyes so she could focus. How was the water? Abbey couldn't find the words; it was as if they were trapped in her throat. She felt like a schoolgirl talking to her first crush.

Finally, Abbey spoke in a whisper. Yes, we meet again. The water is fine. Jamerson came in closer. I cannot hear what you said. The mint from his breath invaded Abbey's space. Do I make you nervous? Absolutely not! Well, Abbey, I don't think that you are being truthful. Why would you say that? Abbey asked. Your body language is saying something very different.

Abbey took a step back, trying to clear her mind. The water is fine. It's not too cold, just right. Jamerson nodded his head. I can say the same about you. Care to take a swim with me? Jamerson asked. No, Abbey said. I have to meet my parents for lunch, maybe next time. So, are you saying I get to see you again? Abbey looked up and replied. "I cannot promise you there will be a next time." Why don't you take my number and call me if you decide to take me up on that swim?

Abbey picked up her cell phone and dialed it into her contact. Abbey contemplated whether to save it or delete it. She'd gathered her belongings just as Jamerson removed his towel from his waist and dove into the water. Damn, milk does that man's body good. Abbey saved Jamerson's number in her contacts and proceeded to the shower.

Abbey arrived at Pearl's Place, a soul food restaurant in Bronzeville. The restaurant has been a staple of the community for over thirty years. The food was mouthwatering. Abbey took a seat in a booth near the window. She and her ex would come here on Sunday for their homemade peach cobbler and vanilla ice cream. Her mind wandered off as she thought about her relationship with him. Did she make the right decision to leave him? She began to contemplate why as her parents approached the table.

Abbey was greeted with a big hug from her mother and a kiss on the forehead by her father. The first question her mother asked was,

"Sunshine, you look a bit thin. Is everything okay?"

Abbey had not told her mom that she was now single. If she had, it would have been this long-drawn-out conversation about her age and when she planned on having children. Dad said," Bev, leave her be. We just got here and haven't sat down". Abbey smiled as a way to say thank you.

Ever since Abbey could remember, her dad was always there to save the day. In Abbey's heart, he was her Superman. There was nothing he wouldn't do for their family. The conversation at the table was full of energy. Beverly and William were over the moon as they spoke about the conference. William had mentioned that he might run for President of his local chapter. Abbey was in awe of her parents. They inspired her, and she dreamed of the day she could meet her life's love.

UNMASK

Abbey had finally made it home. She removed her outerwear, placing it and her gym bag in the foyer closet. As usual, she had a takeout order of a slice of peach cobbler and homemade vanilla ice cream in a container. She made her way to the window facing Lake Michigan. Abbey contemplated whether she would call Jamerson. She did not want him to think she was thirsty. That was a new term she had picked up from her intern, Robyn. The things you learn from the younger generation.

There is nothing wrong with a friendly conversation between two adults. Whom was Abbey trying to convince? She was a grown woman and did not need to explain her actions to anyone. Well, maybe to herself. She had taken a break from the dating scene because she needed to focus on her company. And to find a more meaningful connection in a relationship. No doubt, her ex was everything she wanted initially, but over time, the things that brought them together soon faded. You can say they grew apart. And these things happen. She removed her phone from her pocket and dialed his number.

Chapter 14

FAMILY TIES

After Bryce left, Sal stayed in Arizona to tie up some loose ends with the inspector. He was also able to scout out some more potential properties and investors in the area. Sal had spoken with Lou, and she had decided to cut her trip short by a day since there was not much more she needed to do. Sal called his lawyer to see if there were any updates on the whereabouts of Lou's parents. As Sal expected, there were none. He was saddened that Lou had no idea who she was and where she came from. Sal felt helpless. He needed to do something to help his cousin. He decided to call at least one of the people who could shed some light on this mystery.

Hi, Abuela, it's Sal. How are you? I am doing well for an old lady. Sal laughed. You are still young at heart, Abuela. Sal knew he needed to approach the situation with care. There was still tension between his mother and his Uncle

UNMASK

Eddie. So, he needed to tread lightly.

Abuela, can I ask you a question? Of course, El Nieto. Do you remember a woman named Selena? She was silent for several minutes. Why are you inquiring about her? Abuela asked. Sal took a moment to craft a response that did not seem insensitive. Abuela, I spent the past weekend with Lou. How is Lourdes? She is not doing good. She has been going through a lot. Lou received several letters from Uncle Diego after he died. And in one of those letters, he advised that Selena was Lou's mother.

Abuela, is that true? Salvatore, it seems that your Uncle Diego made good on his promise. What do you mean, Abuela? Sal asked. I remember when Selena arrived at the ranch. She was the only female rancher then and had to prove herself among the other males.

Selena was a tough cookie. She worked just as hard as any man on the crew. Selena was very private and did not share much with anyone. So, it was a surprise when Diego and Selena began spending so much time together.

Diego shared with Abuela his feelings for Selena. The way Diego lit up when she entered the ball that evening. You would have thought he had won the lottery. Shortly after Selena left, Diego became depressed and began drinking heavily. No one knew that Selena was pregnant until Diego came back with Lourdes. Diego insisted that he and Selena were not intimate. And I believed him. Abuela said. Sal could hear a slight tremor in her voice. And he knew he needed to end the call.

Just as he hung up the phone, there was a knock on the door. Sal rose from the chair and took the short walk; he had not ordered room service and was not expecting anyone. When he opened the door, he was surprised to see it was the bartender from two nights ago.

My apologies: I did not mean to disturb you, but I believe I misplaced my bracelet here the other night. Sal stepped aside, allowing her to enter the room. Sal would have welcomed a beautiful woman at his door any other time, but for some reason, this was different.

She immediately pulled back the heavy duvet and the bedding top sheet in search of the bracelet. Sal looked alongside the bed and the floor, but still no luck. He proceeded into the bathroom, and on the counter was a note from the housekeeping staff indicating they had found the bracelet while picking up the soiled towels. He knew the note was not there before.

Sal returned to the bedroom and handed the bracelet to her. She thanked him and asked Sal if he was up for company as she approached the door. He declined her offer and bid her good evening. Sal closed the door and wondered if she had purposely left the bracelet. In his mind, it did not matter; he had other things that were more important than another one-night stand. His mind returned to the conversation with Abuela and knew that something was not adding up with her story, and he would not give up until he found out.

Sal was up early to meet with an investor who had contacted him before he turned in last night. The investor's assistant indicated that A.J. wanted to discuss the property that Sal had viewed with the city inspector on Saturday. Sal agreed to meet at the property at nine that morning.

He arrived at 8:45 and waited for A.J. to arrive. Just as Sal exited the car, an emerald, green Land Rover Evoque with tinted windows and custom twenty-two-inch Seamak satin black with gloss rims pulled up. Sal was not prepared for what he saw when the door opened.

A.J. was not a man as Sal assumed. She exited the vehicle in a Versace sketch baroque cut-out minidress with shoes to match. Her hair was shoulder-length and the color of coal. She approached Sal and extended her hand to greet him. Hello, Mr. De La Cruz. It is a pleasure to meet you. I am Harmony, A.J.'s assistant; we spoke on the phone last night. A.J. should be here momentarily.

As Sal released Harmony's hand, another car pulled into the driveway. The door opened, and Sal anticipated seeing a man exiting the vehicle. Once again, he was mistaken. This time, Sal's mouth immediately fell open. He thought Harmony was beautiful, and she was. But A.J. had a natural beauty that Harmony did not possess. She wore an asymmetric long-sleeve tunic blouse shirt dress with a pair of boot-cut jeans with rips in the knees and some white platform sneakers. Her hair was pulled into a ponytail that complimented her rich toffee skin tone and full face. She wore no make-up, just a hint of lip gloss.

My apologies, Mr. De La Cruz, for my tardiness. I ran into a bit of traffic on the fairway. Sal could detect an accent and needed to figure out where. Please, let's go in and get out of this heat. Sal allowed both Harmony and A.J. to go ahead of him as they entered the dwelling. Sal wiped his brow, and all he could think was that this would be a long meeting.

Chapter 15

DOUBLE-TAKE

C hris had not revealed that Dominique Sanchez had a twin sister named Darcy to Royce. He still needed to determine what evidence Dominique had that indicated the previous DNA sample had been tampered with. Chris was on several notable organizations and committees in the city. And he so happened to be a neighbor to the executive assistant to the Vice President of the Diversity and Inclusion division of the hospital. He reached out to Ursula, and she provided some vital information regarding the recent investigation surrounding the running of several outpatient labs connected to Coventry Memorial Hospital.

Ursula advised that many of the samples collected at the central lab had been tampered with by a disgruntled employee who found out their spouse had been unfaithful. All three children born during the marriage may or may not be biologically his. The employee brought samples to the lab to be tested and inadvertently mislabeled the specimen to cover up the testing for personal reasons. Chris was still not convinced that the sample collected in Royce's case was a part of the specimens in question. Chris asked if she could provide a time frame for the specimen mislabeling. She advised him to give her a week to see what else she could find out.

Loren had called and advised that she had combed Lucas's trail documents again and came across the name of Consuela Rodriguez. Consuela was listed as a CI. (confidential informant) for the prosecutor. This meant that she probably had inside knowledge of the operation firsthand. Chris remembered the D.A. office weighed heavy on her testimony to convict Lucas. He also knew that confidential informants often never take the stand and are placed in the witness protection program for their safety. Chris needed to get ahold of D.A. Morgan to see if he could shed some light on Consuela Rodriguez. He suspects that there may be a connection to the Sanchez sisters.

Chris headed to the office. He needed to grab his case files before going to court. As he approached the building, he had this eerie feeling that someone was following him. As he exited his vehicle, he noticed that an older model Honda Accord had been trailing him since he left the barbershop just before eight this morning. He stopped at the security checkpoint and alerted the police officer of his suspicions. Just as he began to walk away, the individual in the vehicle could be seen on the closed-circuit television pulling into the parking garage. Chris was advised to proceed as normal as the officer radioed his supervisor.

Chris made his way to the elevator. Someone called his name just as he was about to board the car. Chris turned in the direction of the voice and immediately recognized the person. It was Lydia Ross, Bria's attorney. Hey, what are you doing here? Chris asked. I am meeting a colleague. Do you have a second to talk? Both Chris and Lydia boarded the elevator. By now, you have heard about the pending case with Bria and her soon-to-be ex-husband, Nate White. I know about the paternity case, but not the pending divorce. Chris replied.

Lydia advised that Bria contacted her when she received the subpoena; she informed me then. Finally, Chris and Lydia made it to his office. Just as he opened the door, his desk phone began to ring. Chris answered, and it was the police captain indicating that they had apprehended the individual and needed him to come downstairs because the person advised that they were related. Chris was puzzled because he had no relatives who lived in the area. He informed the officer that he would be down shortly.

Lydia indicated that she would give him a call later. But before she left, Chris asked her about Ms. Sanchez's comment regarding the other fathers named in the paternity case. Lydia gave him a raised eyebrow. I was wondering about that as well. I only know of Nate, Royce, and Lucas. Who else could be a potential father? Who knows, Lydia said yet another twist to this saga.

The officer escorted Chris into a small office near the lobby; when the door opened, he was shocked to see who this person was. Chris had not heard from his father since he and his mother divorced when he was nine. Chris was now thirty-seven and dreamt of the day he would see him again. He had rehearsed what he would say but couldn't voice those words today. So, instead, he just stood there, filled with an array of emotions: sadness, anger, hatred, love, and pride.

After his parent's divorce, Chris's mother became his and his brother's, everything from their mother to the disciplinarian, nurse, taxicab driver, counselor, and sole financial supporter. Although Chris and his brother knew it was hard for their mother, she never complained or harbored any ill will toward their father. On the contrary, she always reminded them that we were not the reason for their divorce, but because of their union, it produced the most incredible gift: us. She also told them she loved their father, and sometimes, in a marriage, people can grow apart, which was the case with his parents. At least, that is what his mother told them. But that still did not fill the void Chris had growing up.

Chris could remember the late-night conversations between his mother and father. His mother nearly begged their father to play a more active role in our lives. Explaining that she could not raise a boy into a man; that was his responsibility as their father. It was not as if he had died. In Chris's eyes, he chose to be an absentee father because he knew he was offered the opportunity to have a relationship with him and his brother. After a while, the phone calls stopped, and they no longer asked about him.

The officer asked if Chris knew him. Chris indicated he did but could form the words to say he was his father. Chris replied yes, I know him and walked out the door. Chris wasn't in a suitable head space for this right now. He had to be in court in the next two hours and needed to review the case notes before this trial. As he exited the building, he wondered what he wanted. Was it money or something else? Chris knew he needed to focus before arriving at court.

Chapter 16

PASSING TIME

It felt as if time was at a standstill. It had been two weeks since Leah was placed on the ventilator, and Bryce refused to leave her bedside. Finally, Leah was moved from critical care ICU to step-down as the doctors advised that her lungs had improved enough to start weaning her off the ventilator. Leah's family had arrived in Tennessee shortly after she was admitted and was just as vigilant as Bryce was about her well-being. He spent many hours conversing with her family, especially her father. He also was able to meet Aaron. Bryce could see why he and Leah had been close friends for so long. Royce and Anya were also there, and his parents and Logan had flown in to be a support.

It was another three days before Leah could breathe on her own. But she still had not opened her eyes. Bryce finally went home after much convincing from his mother. Once home, Bryce showered, ate, and lay on the couch. Knowing Leah was not there, he felt uncomfortable sleeping in the bed he shared with her.

Bryce had slept for nearly five hours when he heard his cell phone ring. It was Royce checking in. Before he could ask. Leah is resting, and there is no change. OK, I will be there within the hour. Take your time; there are plenty of us here looking after her. Thanks, bro; I don't know how I would have done this without you all. You never have to thank me for loving and supporting you. That is what was instilled in us. And this is what family does for one another. Bryce rested for another hour before finally packing another overnight bag for the hospital.

He still had yet to eat. Bryce did not have a taste for any more hospital cuisine. So, before arriving back at the hospital, he stopped by one of Leah's favorite Cuban restaurants., He ordered Leah's favorite meal: a Cuban sandwich and fried sweet plantains. It felt like Leah was sitting with him as he ate his dinner. He could hear her distinctive laugh and smell the perfume she wore. Oh, how he missed her and wished she would wake up.

 Bryce finally returned to the hospital, and no one was there when he entered the room. He immediately began to panic. He ran to the nurse's station. Where is Leah Bernard? Bryce asked the young lady who was sitting at the desk. Ms. Bernard was taken to…… before she could finish her sentence, Bryce's mind began to race out of control. He questioned his decision on why he left her side. He could hear a voice say, "I will never leave you." Bryce was too afraid to turn toward the direction of the voice. He wanted to cling to the hope that Leah would never leave him. And she was all right. He began to pray and ask for God's guidance. As he lowered his head, he felt a hand on his shoulder.

Hey bro, are you ok? Bryce turned to face Royce. Where is Leah? She was taken for X-rays. She should be back soon. Man, I thought something terrible had happened to her. Royce looked Bryce directly into his eyes and said," Breath, I know what you are probably thinking. This is not the same situation as Skylar." What happened to her was an accident. Unfortunately, we cannot bring Skylar back, but we still have Leah. I know all of this has been overwhelming and has weighed heavily on your mind. You have to allow yourself to be present at this moment. Take it one minute at a time. We got you! Bryce began to cry because Royce was right. Leah is here, and what a blessing that was in itself. He had placed so many things on his shoulders that it was hard to manage. He finally realized that he was not in this situation by himself.

Another hour passed before transportation returned to the room with Leah. She looked like a princess sleeping. Bryce walked to the head of her bed and gently kissed her lips. He whispered in her ear, 'I love you for eternity." He never thought he could love someone so deeply as he did Leah. As he looked back at the time that they spent together, it was simply amazing. He cradled his hand with hers and distinctively felt her squeeze his hand. Bryce did not want to react prematurely as he did earlier. So, he asked her if she could hear him, please squeeze his hand, and Leah did just as he commanded. Bryce knew that this was a sign that Leah could hear him. And she was slowly coming back to him.

Bryce walked Royce to the elevator and bid him good night. When he returned to the room, he noticed that Leah had repositioned herself in the bed. He began talking to Leah, trying to coax her to move again. No luck. Bryce was still grateful for the progress he had witnessed during the day. Bryce prepared his area for bed. As he did every night, he kneeled by Leah's bed and began to pray. And as he finished, he said AMEN, and so did Leah.

Chapter 17

FILLING IN THE GAP

Anya arrived at the office extra early this morning to prepare for the scheduled interviews on the calendar. In addition, the meeting with Abbey and her executive team was this afternoon. She had been spending more time at the office since Leah's hospitalization. Oh, how she and the others missed seeing her beautiful face in the morning. Anya did not realize how much she depended on Leah as her friend and wing woman. It was Leah who pulled her through so many uphill battles when she was first opening the company. She was so kind and loving when, many times, Anya did not deserve it.

Stacie called, indicating that her first interviewee was waiting for her in the conference room. Anya was impressed as they had arrived fifteen minutes before their scheduled appointment. Anya glanced again at the candidates' resumes before leaving her office to ensure she was prepared. The gentleman rose from his seat when Anya entered the room. He waited for Anya to sit before he took his seat. Then, he extended his hand and introduced himself as Tyler Winters. Tyler was very personable and full of potential and ambition. He was confident and not cocky in his abilities. The only question Anya had for Tyler was why he had applied for this job as it was an entry-level position, and quite frankly, he was overqualified.

Tyler explained that although he was overqualified for the applied position, his current position was no longer the career path he sought, and he needed to be in a more fulfilling job. Anya asked several more questions about the position and its requirements before she ended the interview. Unfortunately, Anya was not convinced Tyler would be the right fit for the job. Although he presents well, she was skeptical that he would stay, especially with the significant reduction in pay he would be offered in this role.

Anya had about an hour before her following interview. She took that time to call Bryce and check on Leah, and he informed her that Leah had spoken her first words last night. Anya was overjoyed. She then called Royce, and he seemed preoccupied as she tried to talk with him. Anya had seen a shift in his mood about three weeks ago, but she attributed that to what was happening with Leah. What worried her the most was that they had not been intimate either. Anya needed a sounding board, so she called her sister Rayn.

Rayn was five years older than Anya and was married with six children. She had recently finished her academic studies last year and decided to take a leave of absence from her job to focus on her family. Rayn was a woman who marched to her own drum, which Anya admired about her. However, their relationship was not as close as Anya would have liked. She believed that it was due to the distance and the age gap. But, in Anya's heart, she knew it was more than that. She credits her therapist, Eileen, now her friend, for allowing her to purge many of her childhood feelings. And get to the root of her problem.

The phone rang several times before Rayn answered. She sounded like she had just run a marathon and was out of breath. Hey sis! I was coming in from the garage when I heard the phone ring. No worries. Do you have time to chat? Of course, I have time for you. Anya explained her dilemma to Rayn, and within seconds, she said, "You just need to talk with him. This has been a very stressful time for both of you. Sis, you must remember that men are creatures of habit and are not the ones who like expressing themselves. Also, you may consider that Royce may still be grieving the loss of his wife and unborn child. Especially now with the events surrounding Leah.

Anya would agree that she and Royce were under stress. But she never considered that this situation could have triggered the loss of Skylar for Royce. But she could see the connection.

Anya and Rayn talked for about another fifteen minutes before their conversation was interrupted by one of her nephews, who yelled out that they were going to be late for work. Anya expressed her love for Rayn and ended the call.

The next candidate had also arrived early, and Anya was equally impressed with their resume. Their skill set and experience were top-notch. Her answer to each question was on point. Anya asked the candidate her last questions before wrapping up the interview.

Miss Lange, how would you describe your relationship with your employer, and why are you looking for another job?

Without hesitation, Miss Lange replied, "I was having an affair with my boss, and his wife found out about us, and now I need to find another job." The answer that Miss Lange gave made Anya gasp for air. She was not expecting that response. Anya made a mental note that she would either eliminate or rephrase that question the next time she conducted an interview. There was no doubt Miss Lange would not be considered for any future positions, and her resume will be marked accordingly in their database.

Anya needed some fresh air after the interviews and her conversation with Rayn. So, she headed to the café for tea and a sandwich. Her mind was all over the place. Was she overthinking all of this? Just as she entered the shop, Abbey called and advised that she needed to reschedule their meeting for next week because of an oversight in scheduling. Anya understood that these things happen. She placed her order and took a seat at her favorite table. Her mind wandered back to the first time she saw Royce here. The vision of him was breathtaking. They had been through a lot this last year, and Anya loved him and needed to know what was happening.

It was almost six when Anya arrived home, and she was surprised to see that Royce was also home. Anya took a moment to gather her thoughts on what she would say to him. Then, she remembered what Rayn had said earlier. Anya walked in and laid her belongings on the table in the foyer. She could smell fried chicken and knew that Royce was preparing something in the kitchen. Anya removed her shoes and proceeded into the kitchen. Royce was standing in the refrigerator as Anya approached him from behind. She wrapped her arms around his waist and laid her head on the middle of his lower back. He felt and smelled so good. Royce placed his hand over hers as they stood there in silence. Finally, they both said simultaneously, "We need to talk." Royce turned around and faced Anya.

Royce appeared nervous as he searched Anya's face to see if he could figure out what she was thinking. Anya walked away and sat at the island as Royce removed the remaining items from the refrigerator. So you go first; what's on your mind Anya asked. Royce seemed to be trying to find the words. Anya, these last few weeks have been tough for me. And we promised one another that we would not keep anything from one another. Royce could see that Anya's demeanor appeared to have changed, as if she was bracing herself.

Anya listened as he spoke; the inflection and intonation in his voice scared her. She could not imagine what he had to say that had him damn near speechless. Was it the grief that had him fighting for the words to express? Royce abruptly stopped and handed Anya a piece of paper that he had retrieved from the back pocket of his slacks. Anya's hand shook as she reached for the paper and laid it on the island. Finally, she closed her eyes and said to herself.

"Lord, please give me the strength to handle what I am about to read."

Chapter 18
PROCEED WITH CAUTION

Sebastián had arrived at Dulles International Airport, awaiting his outgoing flight to France. He was working on an international criminal case with his team and Interpol. This would be Sebastián's first time as the lead investigator on any case. He was ecstatic to have been given such an opportunity, especially at this stage in his career. Sebastián had contacted Ja'Nae last week to inform her that he would be in Europe for an unspecified time. He and Ja'Nae had been communicating more over the past few months and looked forward to reconnecting with her and his family. Sebastián's phone rang, and it was Ocean. He didn't get the chance to see her before leaving the house this morning. Hey, Dad, where are you? I am here in Northern Virginia, waiting to board the plane. He and Ocean chatted for about ten minutes, and then Ocean handed the phone to Marisa. Marisa reviewed her upcoming schedule, which included another overseas assignment to Bangkok. They agreed that Ocean would go since she would be on Spring break. Their call ended just minutes before they announced the boarding of his flight. Sebastián needed this time to regroup and focus on this assignment. He was fully aware of the danger he and his men were facing. So, he had to clear his mind and eliminate unwanted distractions, including Anya.

The flight attendant announced they were finally descending into Heathrow International Airport. Sebastián had not slept much because his mind was entangled in these vivid images of Anya. Anya had tried to call several times after their brief conversation. And soon, the texts and calls ended just like before. Sebastián knew he was acting childish, but he didn't have it in him to be rejected again. He had to snap out of this. There was too much at risk. The team finally reached Lyons, France, just before midnight when they checked into the hotel. The travel was long, and everyone was exhausted. Once in his room, Sebastián called Marisa and then Ma and Pop. He quickly took a hot shower and headed to bed.

The following day, Sebastián met Chief Inspector Wellington, his contact with Interpol, in the hotel lobby to review the case details. Chief Inspector Wellington indicated that the agency became involved when customs seized a large quantity of drugs and firearms at Gatwick Airport. Unfortunately, there was no way to trace the guns and drugs to anyone. That was not until one of his agents received a tip from a confidential informant who provided information on several individuals with close ties with the Cypress Motorcycle Club, whose headquarters was out of Nashville. The informant advised that another shipment would arrive in the next two weeks, and one of the big bosses would supervise that transaction. Chief Inspector Wellington handed the case files to Sebastián and said he would send him and his team a car within the hour.

As promised, a car arrived at the hotel, and they were driven to Interpol headquarters. Upon arriving, the team was escorted to a large conference room with heavily tinted windows. The room had little décor besides the multi-com phone in the center of the mahogany table. Chief Inspector Wellington entered the room and quickly went to work. He introduced his team and their roles in this case. Sebastián was asked to do the same. Just as the meeting was about to end, an older gentleman entered the room and asked to speak with Chief Inspector Wellington. The gentleman had a presence that spoke volumes. Sebastián took note of how Chief Inspector Wellington's demeanor changed. Sebastián could only think he was his boss or one of the higher-ranking officers here at Interpol. Nevertheless, the exchange between the men ended before it began.

Sebastián exited the conference room and was enroute to the elevator when a beautiful female headed his way. Sebastián was about to pass her. She stopped him and asked for directions to the conference room. Her French accent took him aback. Sebastián was speechless as he pointed in the direction of the room. Just as she began to walk away, Chief Inspector Wellington approached from the opposite direction. Special Agent Moreau, I am glad you found time in your busy day to join us. I see that you have met Investigator Collins. No, I have not. But he was kind enough to point me toward the conference room.

Special Agent Moreau extended her hand toward Sebastián. Her beauty still awed him, and the accent drove him crazy. Sebastián finally found his voice when Agent Moreau snapped her fingers before his face. My apologies that we were not officially introduced. It is a pleasure to meet you. I am pleased that everyone knows one another, Chief Inspector Wellington said. Because you two will be partnering together as we work on this case. Both Sebastián and Special Agent Moreau look at one another in disbelief. We don't have time to be gawking at one another. Chief Inspector Wellington said. I suggest you get something to eat, Investigator Collins; please get Special Agent Moreau up to speed on the details of this case.

Sebastián pressed the down button for the elevator. The doors opened, and as the doors were about to close, Special Agent Moreau got on. I know a good place that serves a great patty and chips. Sebastián gave Special Agent Moreau a side-eye. She immediately began to laugh. My apologies: you are an American: hamburgers and fries. And please call me Alex. Special Agent Moreau is so overrated and formal. I am Sebastián. They exited on the ground level of the parking deck. Sebastián followed Alex as she made her way to her vehicle. Sebastián laughed hard, making Alex stop dead in her tracks. What have you so amused Alex said.? So, this must be your Sage. No, it is he, and his name is Savage. So, am I to guess that you have a bike too? Yes, I do. That is smashing, Alex said. I mean, great. The bistro is only meters from here, so we can walk. I need to grab my tele. They proceeded to the restaurant, less than ten minutes from headquarters.

Sebastián looked up at the neon sign in the window: "Rem's Pub." They serve American cuisine. Alex said. They have the best food here. This is where I go when I have a taste for some late-night authentic coronary-clogging food. My type of place, Sebastián said. They took a seat at the counter. The waitress brought them their menus and said something in French to Alex, and she looked over her shoulder and smiled. Sebastián would not dare to ask what she asked and Alex's reply.

They finished their meal and headed back to the office. By the time they returned, the others had left. Alex suggested we call it a day and meet in the morning at seven. Sebastián agreed. In doing so, he realized he had no way back to the hotel. Alex saw the puzzled look in his eyes and immediately removed her extra helmet from her satchel bag at the bike's rear. Sebastián hopped on, and away they went.

Chapter 19

PUTTING IN THE WORK

Leah lay motionless in bed, afraid to move despite her brain telling her to. She could hear people talking, but their voices were muffled and unclear. Suddenly, the room fell silent, and she could only hear Bryce's voice. She could feel his presence and listen to him praying, asking God to bring her back to him. Bryce's voice slowly fades away. Leah is enveloped by the sweet scent of morning dew mixed with honeysuckle and wild lavender. She now hears the laughter of children playing in the distance and a woman calling them in for supper. It is her mother's voice that she hears. Leah patiently waited for her name to be called; by now, all the children had gone in, and it was just her.

Suddenly, memories of her childhood came rushing back to her. She sees images of her siblings and father pushing her mother on a swing in their backyard. The love they shared was magical. The photos stop, and her mother embraces her in her arms. Leah weeps as her mother tells her she has much more to do and many people who love and need her. But she would be with her always. Leah could feel herself drifting back into a peaceful sleep.

The chirping of birds awoke Leah from her sleep. She slowly opened her eyes, and the vibrant colors of the sun unmasked the beautiful rainbow hidden in the clouds' blankets. She turned her head toward the sounds of a soft snore and the wrestling of heavy blankets. Then, finally, a head emerged from under the off-white blanket. Leah recognized her man before he turned to adjust himself on the uncomfortable recliner that served as his bed. He stretched, removed the blanket, and headed for what Leah assumed was the bathroom. Leah tried to speak, but nothing came out. It was as if her vocal cords were paralysis. Her throat was sore and dry. She needed some water. Her eyes scanned the room and landed on a mauve-colored container at the foot of the bed, accompanied by disposable cups. Despite feeling weak, she managed to reposition herself in bed and grabbed onto the rail to sit up. The beautiful Afghan blanket that covered her legs was removed as she pushed herself to the edge of the bed. Her legs dangled as she reached again for the rail to raise herself, and then suddenly, the alarms began to blare, piercing her eardrums. Bryce appeared in the doorway of the bathroom, wearing just a towel. Startled by Leah's sudden presence, he dropped the towel, exposing him. Leah was taken aback as Bryce hurriedly approached her, falling to his knees and expressing his gratitude to God for her safe return. As he stood up, several people entered the room, and Bryce was unaware that he was unclothed until a nurse handed him a blanket. It was evident that Bryce was not shy as he proceeded to the bathroom to get dressed.

The team swiftly attended to Leah, carefully placing her back in a lying position on the bed. A nurse promptly assessed her vital signs and urgently requested that the on-call provider be contacted immediately. Bryce bombarded the nurses with numerous questions, making it difficult for them to keep up with his rapid pace. The clinical team firmly directed Bryce to wait in the hallway while they tended to Leah.

The room was chaotic. Leah was being poked and prodded as she was being asked several questions.

Does anything hurt?

Do you know your name?

Do you know where you are?

Who is the President of the United States?

Leah knew the answer but had no voice to verbalize her responses. So, the nurse advised Leah to nod her head when she said the correct answer to the questions. After several minutes, the doctor completed his assessment and asked the nurse to have Bryce come in.

Bryce quickly entered the room after being summoned by the nurse and saw Leah sitting in the chair next to the bed. He was moved to tears by her stunning beauty. He knew how much Leah had gone through, but she still could smile. He immediately went to her and held her hand. Leah squeezed Bryce's hand to let him know that she was okay. The doctor informed Bryce that Leah was on the road to a full recovery but cautioned that she would need physical therapy to regain strength in her lower extremities due to immobility. In addition, her voice will not immediately return after removing the intubation tube, as her vocal cords require time to heal.

As the doctor left the room, Leah gently squeezed Bryce's hand and mouthed that she was hungry. To their surprise, both Bryce and the doctor let out a laugh. Then, jokingly, Bryce said, "Doc, if you don't want to see this beautiful lady turn into a monster, I suggest you get her something to eat." The doctor took notice and gave specific instructions to Leah's nurse, requesting that a speech pathologist assess her before consuming solid foods. Leah and Bryce remained silent, exchanging nothing but deep gazes. Finally, after what felt like an eternity, a single teardrop fell from Leah's eye as she attempted to speak. Without hesitation, Bryce knelt before her and rested his head on her lap, knowing no words were necessary.

CHAPTER 20
HIDDEN EXPECTATIONS

Abbey had just wrapped up her last call for the evening when Craig knocked on her door. Are you headed out Abbey asked, Yeah, Craig answered, " I just wanted to see if you needed anything. No, I'm about to leave out, too. I can wait Craig said. Okay. Abbey turned off the computer and grabbed her bag.

Craig inquired about the meeting with Anya as they both entered the elevator. It has been postponed as there was a family emergency that Anya needed to take care of first. And there was a scheduling error on our behalf. Have you considered the potential conflict arising from your partnership with Anya, as I previously mentioned? We can handle keeping our personal and business matters separate, considering our maturity. Craig picked up on a negative attitude and promptly changed the topic of the conversation.

Do you have plans for tonight? I do Abbey replied as they exited the elevator. Craig could tell that Abbey was not in a talkative mood. OK, have a good time. After bidding Craig a good night, Abbey approached her vehicle.

It had taken Abbey nearly two weeks to build up the confidence to make that call. She debated whether to contact her ex, try to salvage their relationship, or move on. In the end, Abbey chose to reach out to Jamerson instead.

Abbey felt nervous as she started dialing Jamerson's number. Finally, she hung up and took a few deep breaths to calm down before redialing the number. "Hello, Abbey," came the voice on the second ring. The apparent anticipation of her call took Abbey aback. She consciously tried to remain open-minded and avoid jumping to conclusions before the conversation started. And she was glad she did because they talked for over three hours. Jamerson was a remarkable man with a well-rounded personality and a penchant for travel. He was highly educated and possessed a thought-provoking mind. And let's not forget that he was also quite handsome. Nevertheless, Abbey opted not to ask Jamerson what he did for a living as it was too presumptuous. And he did not ask what she did for a living either.

Abbey arrived home around seven and planned to meet Jamerson for drinks at The Berkshire Room at nine. After showering, Abbey wore her curve-fitting bootcut camouflage jeans and black cami. She paired them with an open-front White cable knit longline cardigan and black wedge boots. She accessorized with gold hooped earrings and applied light glitter lip gloss to complete her outfit.

The Uber driver pulled up to the restaurant just before nine. Abbey decided not to drive because she found parking on Michigan Ave. Friday night can be difficult. She paid the driver and proceeded into the establishment. This was

Abbey's first time here. The atmosphere was laid back with a grown-folk flare. She had checked them out on Yelp and was pleased to see they had received excellent reviews. The restaurant was crowded as patrons waited to be seated. Abbey felt her phone vibrate in her cross-body bag. It was Jamerson calling, but she couldn't hear him, so she stepped outside to take the call. "I'm sorry, I didn't catch what you said; I had to step out," she explained. I can hear you just fine. Abbey looked up, and Jamerson stood a few feet from her. He laughed and said, "We must stop running into each other like this." Anya also laughed, and they headed back into the restaurant.

The hostess led them to their table, and Jamerson kindly pulled out her chair, waiting until Abbey was seated before taking his seat like a gentleman. Abbey felt nervous and started fidgeting with the napkin, struggling to find the right words. She found conversing with Jamerson on the phone more manageable than in person. Jamerson noticed Abbey was struggling to speak, so he initiated and started the conversation.

'"Would you consider yourself a foodie?" Jamerson asked.

Abbey responded, "Yes, I do."

Jamerson inquired, "So you're not someone who only eats salads, are you?"

Abbey chuckled, "No, and I don't mind eating with my hands."

Jamerson recommended, "Well, this place has an excellent seafood boil.

Would you like me to order it with extra crab legs?"

Yes, and can I also have an extra boiled egg?

Abbey felt more at ease and slowly relaxed.

As their food was served, Jamerson turned to Abbey and suggested, "You can still back out if you'd like." To which Abbey gracefully declined. However, she requested the waiter bring a bib for Jamerson because she did not want him to ruin his nice shirt.

The evening was delightful, full of laughter and discoveries. Jamerson was a refreshing presence, and they chatted so much that the waiter had to remind them that the restaurant was closing in ten minutes.

Abbey was about to call an Uber after leaving the restaurant, but Jamerson stopped her. He felt it was too late for her to wait for a ride and offered to take her home instead. Abbey appreciated his directness and concern for her safety.

Jamerson arrived at Abbey's place; there was a brief silence. He then asked Abbey if she would accompany him on another date. Abbey didn't hesitate and said yes. Jamerson was a gentleman and helped Abbey out of the car. He kissed her gently on the cheek and warmly embraced her as she entered the building.

Abbey realized it was too early to conclude whether there was a connection with Jamerson. Nevertheless, she could confidently say this was one of the most enjoyable dates she had experienced in a long time.

CHAPTER 21

LATE NIGHT CONVERSATION

The alarm rang, waking Sal from his sleep. He slowly opened his eyes, yawned, and then stretched. He closed his eyes again, allowing his mind to reconstruct the image of A.J. She was gorgeous, and he wanted to know everything about her, including what A. J. stood for. Sal lay there for another ten minutes before getting up to shower.

After showering, he headed to the kitchen to prepare breakfast and a pot of coffee. Sal checked his planner on his phone and had multiple meetings scheduled. He called his assistant, Jaz, and asked that she remove his meetings with Bryce until further notice.

Since Leah's hospitalization, Sal has regularly communicated with Bryce and was thrilled to learn she is recovering well. Despite a busy schedule upon returning from Arizona, Sal remains committed to finding Lou's parents. However, Abuela is uncooperative and won't provide any additional information. Sal contacted his lawyer again, but unfortunately, no helpful information was obtained.

Upon arriving at the office, Sal was warmly welcomed by Jaz, who promptly handed him the contract required for his first meeting. He glanced at the document just before he entered the boardroom. Clarke and Margo Fontaine were no strangers to the real estate market. They had purchased several properties in the past from Sal. Margo Fontaine was a confident and articulate woman who possessed beauty, intelligence, talent, and charisma. She also comes from money and has no problem with spending it. On the other hand, Clarke displayed a greater level of restraint. Although reserved, it did not hinder his ability to be very observant regarding business transactions. Today's meeting felt strange. Margo was very chatty and aggressive, which was out of her character. She made several sexually explicit comments, which made Sal feel very uncomfortable. Sal firmly believes Clarke enjoyed observing Margo's blatant flirtation with another man.

When Sal's phone rang and he saw that it was Lou calling, he was relieved. He saw this as an opportunity to end their meeting earlier. He excused himself and had Jaz finish up the paperwork with the Fontaine.

Sal sensed that something was amiss during his conversation with Lou. She finally indicated she was upset about receiving a letter that confused and troubled her. To try and get to the bottom of things, Lou reached out to the hospital where she was born. To her surprise, they informed her that they had no record of her birth despite her possession of a birth certificate.

Sal found this highly perplexing and urged Lou to send the birth certificate to him overnight so that he could pass it on to his attorney for further investigation. He assured Lou he would do everything he could to help her locate her parents. He could hear the relief in Lou's voice as they ended their call.

Sal arrived at the Capital Grille at six o'clock to meet his mother for a late dinner after failing to reach his Abuela. When Rosa Marie De La Cruz entered the restaurant, Sal was struck by her stunning beauty, from her shoulder-length brown hair to her toned physique and radiant complexion. It wasn't easy to guess her age. Many people believed her to be Sal's girlfriend. or sister. Sal stood up as she approached the table, embracing her warmly to convey how much he had missed her. Without warning, Rosa berated Sal with numerous questions, many of which were in Spanish, which he could not decipher. He could only shake his head. He kissed her on her cheek to call a truce, as he knew they had not spoken in over a month due to his busy schedule.

Madre, I apologize for not calling you despite being busy. Please forgive me. Just like when he spoke to his Abuela, he had to be careful with what he said. Madre, can I ask you something? Sure, Mijo, you can ask me anything. Have you ever heard Abuelo or Abuela speak of a woman named Selena? Yes, I have. I heard others mention her also. I recall how Uncle Diego would become animated when discussing her. Uncle Diego was older than Selena and made it clear to the other men on the ranch that she was not to be pursued. It was obvious that he was in love with her. Do you remember when Uncle Diego left the ranch? No Mijo. I was away at school then, and when I returned that summer, Rissa had already given birth.

Sal realized his mother was unaware that Lou was not her biological niece. This left Sal feeling quite perplexed as to how this could be possible. The secrecy surrounding the matter only increased his confusion. Sal's determination to uncover the truth grew stronger. He felt that going to Colorado was the only way he could progress with this.

Later that evening, Sal planned to call his younger brother Matteo. Matteo was seven years younger than Sal. He and Sal's relationship was close, more like a father-son relationship. Sal and Matteo's father died of kidney disease when Matteo was five. After they relocated to Florida, our visits to the ranch were few and far between. We may be visited every two years. That was not until Matteo chose to attend the University of Colorado and pursue a degree in bioengineering. This afforded Matteo more time with our grandparents and the rest of the family. After graduating, Matteo was offered a job in his field and moved to Denver. Matteo's career had him traveling the globe, and it was never a shock when he called and said he was out of the country on business. It was a long shot, but Sal was running out of options. Maybe Matteo can shed some light on this mystery.

It was late when Sal made it home. He had driven his mother home after dinner and stayed longer than expected. Rosa convinced him to come in for some dessert. The dessert was another word for being nosy. During their conversation, Sal's mom was intrusive by prying into his personal life. Sal wasn't comfortable discussing such matters with her.

Nonetheless, their chat triggered a recollection of A.J. in Sal's memory. He wanted to reach out to her but did not want to come across as being pushy. Even though he felt annoyed by the conversation, he understood that his mother had no intention of causing any harm.

Sal called his brother Matteo and patiently waited for him to pick up. After a few rings, Matteo answered with a warm greeting. "Hey there, little bro!

It's been a while since we last spoke," Sal replied. Matteo was curious about the call and asked, "What's on your mind? Why the late-night call?" Matteo inherited his father's no-nonsense approach, a trait also shared by Sal.

Sal informed Matteo about the details of Lou's paternity issues. Matteo mentioned that he had recently been to the ranch, and Abuela had asked him to clean out Uncle Diego's house, which had been vacant since he died. However, it still appeared as if someone had been living in it. Matteo advised that there was food in the refrigerator and that the bed had been slept in. The. brothers made plans to meet up with one another in a week.

After hanging up with Matteo, Sal replayed his conversation with his mom in his head. When he asked about Uncle Diego's return to the ranch, he noticed something strange about her response. Rosa mentioned that she had just returned from school for the summer but also brought up Aunt Rissa's recent birth of Lou without being prompted. Sal wondered why she mentioned the baby without being asked about it. Had she talked with Abuela? Or does she know more than she is saying?

CHAPTER 22

UNEXPECTED ENCOUNTERS

Sebastián has been running on only ten hours of sleep over the past seven days. The entire team has been working nonstop, trying to devise a plan to intercept the shipment of drugs and weapons that the confidential informant had told them would arrive in less than a week. Sebastián knows the plan must be perfect as he has much at stake. The informant gave them the name of Rex Slaughter, the person in charge of the shipment. Alex searched for the name in the Interpol database, but it came back as belonging to a deceased person. Sebastian contacted Captain Reynolds with the detective bureau, and they found a hit on the name in their database. To their surprise, Rex Slaughter was alive and well, and his identity had been stolen. According to the court documents, the person using Mr. Slaughter's name and credit cards was not a male but a female named Josie Afton.

UNMASK

According to Captain Reynold, Josie had gone missing eight months ago. However, he suspects she may have been placed in the witness protection program due to her involvement with money laundering and an international drug cartel. Upon entering Josie Afton's name into the Interpol database, Alex found a long list of charges dating back to her teenage years. Additionally, she was able to acquire a recent photo of Josie. The informant was shown a picture of Josie, but they could not identify her as having any connections with Rex Slaughter. But was adamant that Rex was a male and existed.

Chief Inspector Wellington enlisted the help of a forensic artist to create a composite sketch of the individual in question. The drawing was subsequently fed into the facial recognition software, successfully identifying the suspect as Desmond 'Styles" Arrington. Mr. Arrington was tied to a drug cartel in Arkansas and Tennessee. He frequents strip, motorcycle, and gentlemen's clubs in those areas. The picture of Desmond 'Styles" Arrington was given to the informant, who positively identified him as Rex Slaughter.

Sebastián was elated that they now had a face to this individual. The team obtained additional information on Styles to include prominent players in the operation. One is a former state trooper serving time at the Federal Correctional Institution in Memphis. Captain Reynolds said he would dig deeper into this and get back to him.

It was getting late, the team was functioning on fumes, and everyone was on edge. Tomorrow was set to be even more demanding than today. On his way to the hotel, Sebastián decided to stop at the nearby restaurant. He ordered a burger, fries, coke, and a slice of carrot cake. Just as he was about to leave, Alex arrived and collected her to-go order from the counter. Sebastián joked, "Looks like we both needed some artery-clogging food." They both laughed. I needed that, Alex said. It has been a long day, Sebastián said. Yes, it has.

"Did you walk here Sebastián asked?" Yes, I did. I can give you a ride back to the parking garage; it is too late for you to be walking. They drove the short distance back to the office. Sebastián opened the door to his rental and waited until Alex had made it to her motorcycle. Sebastián yelled out and asked if she needed a ride home since it had been a long day and eleven at night. Alex did not immediately respond. Yes, that would be nice. I am tired and forgot to bring my satchel to carry the food in.

Sebastián watched as Alex secured her bike and headed to the car. Alex suggested that she drive since she was unsure if Sebastián would know the area. By the time they reached Alex's flat, Sebastián was fast asleep. Alex gently nudged him to wake him. But he did not budge. After several hard nudges, Sebastián woke up. Alex knew he could not drive, so she offered for him to stay the night.

The following day, Sebastián woke up to the delicious aroma of coffee and bacon. He could hear someone bustling around in the kitchen, and he assumed it was Alex. However, he paused for a moment to consider his thoughts. He wasn't sure if Alex was single or taken, and he couldn't recall seeing a ring on her finger. Plus, she never mentioned personal details about herself, and their conversations were always about the case. Being a police officer, Sebastian was always careful not to share too much information. Sebastián stretched and removed the blanket laid neatly across his large frame. He sat up and looked out the picture window. It was still dark outside. He pulled his phone from his jacket that he still had on. It was almost six. He rose from the couch and headed down the hallway leading to the kitchen. On the wall hung some beautiful artwork, including several wooden masks and black and white photos.

"Good morning," Alex greeted Sebastián as he entered the kitchen. "I hope you slept well. Would you like some coffee?"

"Yes, I did," Sebastián replied. "I'll take a cup."

Alex handed Sebastián a cup of coffee. There is sugar and cream on the table. Thanks, I prefer my coffee black. I also made some bacon and was about to scramble eggs and pop some toast in the toaster. Would you like a plate? Yes, please.

Can you point me in the direction of your restroom? It's down the hall and the first door on the left. If needed, you'll find clean towels under the sink and an extra toothbrush. Thank you.

After freshening up, Sebastián returned to the kitchen where his food awaited. He sat, bowed his head, and said a prayer over his meal. Alex was impressed by his gesture, even though she wasn't religious. She appreciated the gratitude.

"Hey, did you take these stunning photos on the wall?" asked Sebastián. "Yes, I did," replied Alex. "Thank you for the compliment.

How long have you been taking pictures?

I started taking photos by chance in college. I needed an elective class and chose photography. I've been hooked ever since." Sebastián praised Alex for her exceptional attention to detail and skill in the craft.

They finished their breakfast, and Alex cleared the table. Sebastián offered to wash the dishes before leaving for the hotel. They arrived at the entrance to the hotel. Sebastián suggested that Alex take the car, and he would get a ride to the office with one of his team members. Alex quickly responded that a vehicle was on the way to get her. Sebastián did not protest and said, "I will see you at the office." Sebastián waited until the vehicle arrived to pick up Alex, then proceeded up to his room to take a shower and onto the office.

Sebastián arrived at the office a little before eight. The teams had gathered in the conference room for an urgent operational meeting. Chief Inspector Wellington and the gentleman Sebastian had noticed the first day at Interpol came in. Their facial expression was stoic, indicating that the matter at hand was likely to be serious.

Good morning, everyone; please let me introduce you all to L.J. Baxter, Head of Criminal Investigation. Chief Inspector Wellington turns the podium over to Mr. Baxter. His voice commanded our attention as he spelled the case out in depth. He informed the team that agents would be stationed at all the major airports, Charles de Gaulle, Orly, and Beauvais, and train stations covering the route from London to Paris. He also enlisted the help of the National Police here in France and The Metropolitan Police Service in London.

At the direction of Mr. Baxter, Chief Inspector Wellington was tasked with assigning teams to various locations. As anticipated, Alex and Sebastián were placed on a team with Riff, an Interpol agent, and Ace, one of the three criminologists involved in the case.

Sebastián was impressed with Mr. Baxter, but he wasn't sure if it was because of his sheer confidence or because he was a man of color. Nevertheless, he left a positive footprint in his mind. The meeting lasted another four hours before the team was dismissed for the day. This was a welcome surprise and would allow for some well-needed sleep.

UNMASK

As everyone exited the room, Sebastián approached Alex and asked if she had any plans for today, and she instantly advised no. Sebastián suggested dinner and a tour of the city. Alex agreed, and they made plans to meet later that evening.

CHAPTER 23

BOMBSHELL

The past week has been hectic for Chris, with court cases, new clients, and a surprise visit from Daniel still weighing heavily on his mind. He had no idea why he decided to visit him as they hadn't spoken since his parent's divorce, and Chris had no desire to have a relationship with him at this point in his life. He knew that if he told his mother, she would try to convince him to talk with him, which was not something Chris was willing to do.

Chris was up and out of the house early this morning. He finally had the opportunity to speak with D.A. Morgan; he was able to provide some missing pieces to the puzzle. In their conversation, D.A. Morgan indicated that Consuela Rodriguez was given immunity in exchange for her testimony, which Chris had suspected. But what he did not expect was this bombshell.

UNMASK

Consuela Rodriguez was not just an informant but an undercover agent working for one of the federal bureaus.

 D.A. Morgan stated that he was not at liberty to provide any further information and was not sure if he should be divulging such sensitive information as this to him. Chris understood the predicament that D.A. Morgan was placing himself in and appreciated the information he had been given.

It was late afternoon when Chris arrived at the office. He stopped by Royce's office to fill him in on the newest development and see if he had scheduled his appointment for the paternity test. However, he was surprised to learn that Royce had taken a personal day and would be in tomorrow.

Chris proceeds to his office, and just as he is about to sit down, Loren comes in with an arm full of files.

Hello, Mr. Calloway. I hope you don't mind, but I continued to search for additional information on Ms. Sanchez. I ran an inquiry on all the cases she was involved with, and the one thing they all had in common was human trafficking. Ms. Sanchez has worked on several pro bono cases involving the victims for the last four years. Chris was shocked as Loren provided details of what she had found. But what intrigued him the most was why Dominique was taken on these types of cases.

Chris thanked Loren for her hard work as she handed the files over to him.

Do you need anything else, Mr. Calloway, before I leave for lunch?

No, Chris responded. Take the rest of the day off.

Are you sure? Yes. Thanks, Mr. Calloway. See you in the morning.

Loren paused before leaving and advised that Lydia Ross had called several times and requested that he call her as soon as possible.

Chris placed a call to the florist and ordered a lovely floral arrangement for Loren as a way to say thank you for her hard work. He scheduled the delivery for tomorrow just before Loren arrived at work.

His next call was to Lydia. Hi, I got your message; it sounded urgent. Chris could hear Lydia take a deep breath. I have been unable to make contact with Bria. The mail sent to her was returned from the address her office had on file.

When was the last time you spoke to her?

A few days before, I ran into you at your office.

Lydia sounded very concerned about the safety of Bria and Mia and suggested that they schedule a meeting with Nate's attorney.

After ending his call with Lydia, Chris immediately dialed Dominique Sanchez's office number. As he expected, it went directly to voicemail. Chris dialed the number to the General District Court and confirmed that Dominique was on the docket for a pre-trail hearing tomorrow at nine; Chris had a disposition scheduled for tomorrow at ten in the same building. He will look for her while he is there.

Chris opted to end his day early and work from home. He gathers the case files for tomorrow's disposition along with the files given to him by Loren. He still wondered why Dominique was taking on these human trafficking cases. The case with Lucas and Bria did involve suspicion of human trafficking. Chris could see why Dominique had an interest in the case. But it still didn't make sense because she is a family law attorney.

He spotted the rack card on the bookcase he had picked up at Dominique's office. Chris remembered the conversation with Misha Saunders and recalled her saying that Dominique and her family had fled from Cuba after her father was killed. Could this be the reason?

Chris needed answers, and the only one that could answer them was Dominique.

CHAPTER 24

DECISIONS

Anya had not slept well since her conversation with Royce a week ago. She had been avoiding him since then, feeling that the letter he had given her could change the trajectory of their relationship. She entered the kitchen, and the letter was still on the island. Anya picked it up. Her heart began to race uncontrollably as she read through its contents. The letter caught her off-guard, leaving her with a flurry of emotions. Anya couldn't help but wonder why this was happening again, especially with someone as messy and deceitful as Bria. Anya placed the letter back on the island. She then called Stacie to let her know she would be in after lunch.

Anya had no idea where she was going. All she knew was that she needed space and time to clear her mind. Anya had been driving aimlessly for over an hour. Before she knew it, she was less than a mile from Sebastián's farmhouse. Anya took the exit without thinking. She had no clue what she would say to him. The last time Anya had spoken to Sebastián was when Leah had passed out in her office. Although Anya had attempted to contact him since then, he had not returned her calls or texts.

It had been over a year since Anya had been to the farmhouse. She was astonished at how beautiful it was. Sebastián had added an iron-wrought gate and a dual staircase, giving the house a charming appeal. She remembers the first time Sebastián brought her here and how he made her feel. Anya sat in her thoughts and wondered what her life would have been like if she had pursued a relationship with Sebastián.

The gate began to open, startling Anya. She could see a figure in the distance walking her way. Anya started her car and began to back up until she heard her name being called.

Ms. McMichael, is that you?

Anya looked again and realized it was Mr. Thomas. Anya stopped the car as Mr. Thomas approached.

Anya let down her passenger window and greeted him. What brings you out this way? Anya did not know how to respond. "I had some business out this way and needed to use the restroom."

Come on in; I was making breakfast and could use some company.

Mr. Thomas waited on the porch as Anya gathered her items from the car. Anya climbed the stairs and entered the house. It was warm and cozy, as she remembered. The walls were no longer bare. They now had beautiful artwork hanging throughout the family room and a portrait of Ocean over the mantel.

There were pictures on the sofa table of Mrs. Margaret and another woman Anya assumed was his mother. But what caught her attention was a photo of Sebastián, Ocean, and a beautiful woman. Could this be Ocean's mother? I can take your coat, Ms. McMichael, while you go to the bathroom. Anya had forgotten she told Mr. Thomas her reason for stopping by.

Thank you, and please call me Anya.

Anya entered the bathroom, and as she stood looking at herself in the mirror, she felt a bit jealous as she thought about the woman in the photo with Sebastián. What would her life be like if Royce were Mia's father? Left out and alone.

Anya felt herself becoming anxious. Her palms of hands began to sweat. She turned on the faucet and splashed cool water on her face and neck. The room started to spin. Anya immediately sat on the floor with her back against the door. She began to take deep, cleansing breaths through her nose and out through her mouth. She repeated it several more times before she felt herself relaxing. She took a few more breaths before she stood up.

There was a knock on the door. Ms. McMichael, are you ok?

Anya steadies her voice before speaking. Yes, Mr. Thomas, I am fine. Ok, breakfast is ready; you don't want it to get cold.

I will be out shortly. And it's Anya. Yes, Ms. McMichael.

Anya could only laugh as she wiped away her tears and freshened her face. She applied a thin layer of lip gloss and anxiously headed to the kitchen. Upon entering the kitchen, Anya was greeted by the delightful aroma of cinnamon. Mr. Thomas quickly pulled out a chair for her and graciously offered her a napkin. As she suspected, Mr. Thomas had prepared a feast fit for royalty.

"Wow, Mr. Thomas, that smells incredible. What delicious creation have you prepared for us?" Anya inquired enthusiastically.

Ms. McMichael.

Mr. Thomas, please call me Anya. We're friends, and friends don't use formal titles. Ok, Anya.

I have cinnamon pecan waffles, scrambled eggs, maple bacon, sausage, hash browns, freshly squeezed lemonade, and orange juice.

Now that is a spread! I cannot drive home if I try to eat all this food. Is Sebastián coming out to the house today? No, he, Ocean, and Marisa are out of the country. I am not sure when they will be back. They have traveled quite a bit since Marisa and Ocean moved in last year.

Anya said, "It sounds like you have a full house." Yes, I do. I have seen a change in Sebastian since they arrived. He is happier now. At one point, I was very concerned about him."

I am glad he is back to his old self.

After Anya finished her breakfast, Mr. Thomas took her on a tour of the grounds. The views were breathtaking. He introduced her to Sage, their new fowl.

Anya was flatter that Sebastian remembered the name she had selected for her motorcycle. What a unique name for such an animal.

Yes, it is replied, Mr. Thomas. Sebastian mentioned he named her after someone extraordinary.

Anya and Mr. Thomas continued their walk on the grounds. Afterward, Mr. Thomas packed Anya a to-go bag filled with items from breakfast, homemade maple syrup, and a slice of pecan pie that he had baked earlier that morning, Anya hugged and thanked Mr. Thomas for his hospitality. As Anya settled in her car to drive away, she heard Mr. Thomas say I hope to see you soon, Anya.

Anya waved and, in her mind, knew that she would not because Sebastian had moved on.

Anya made it back into the city just before noon. She called Stacie to let her know she would not be in and was going to visit Leah. It had been a few days since she had visited.

Anya stopped in the gift shop to purchase some items for Leah. She picked up some candy, a pair of pajamas, slippers, undergarments, a magazine, and a book that caught her eye named UNMASK.

When Anya entered the room, Leah was asleep, and Bryce was too. She quietly placed the items in the chair next to the bed. Anya retrieved a pen from her purse and left a note for Leah;

My Beautiful Friend,
I did not want to wake you or Bryce. Here are some items that I am sure you

can use. I will return later to see you. We have some catching up to do. XOXO

Anya

Anya had no desire to go home. So, she drove to the pier and sat on a bench facing the lake. She took out the book she had purchased from the gift shop and began reading.

Her phone rang, interrupting her as she finished chapter four; it was Terri. Hi Anya. The property you were interested in is still on the market. When are you planning to come down to see it?

Terri, can I give you a call in a couple of days? By then, I will know what direction I am going in.

Anya knew she needed to have a heartfelt talk with Royce when she got home. But until then, she continued to read her book and enjoy the tranquility and beautiful river views.

CHAPTER 25

LIFE

It had only been seven days since Leah had awoken from an induced coma and was gradually regaining her memory of the past month. She watched as Bryce slept peacefully beside her. Leah was grateful, feeling blessed to have such a fantastic man in her life.

Leah was on the road to recovery. She started physical and occupational therapy five days ago. Her legs felt like wet noodles when she first stood. The doctor said it would feel that way due to her immobility. The therapists were also impressed with her progress. But they also reminded her there was no need to rush; take it slow because her body still needed time to heal.

A knock at the door causes Bryce to wake up.

UNMASK

Foodservice, can I come in? Leah answered in a whisper. Come in. The male attendant entered and placed the food on the bedside table at the end of the bed. Bryce rose from the recliner chair to assist Leah. Bryce adjusted the table across the bed in front of Leah. He removed the lid as Leah repositioned herself in the bed.

The speech pathologist cleared Leah, and she could now eat solid foods. Bryce looked at Leah's facial expression as she stared at the meal before her. Before Leah could get a word out, Bryce quickly said, "You want something else to eat?" Leah laughed, "Yes, please."

OK, what do you have a taste for? Leah smiled. I want, a Cuban sandwich, French fries, spring egg roll, shrimp fried rice, and strawberry soda.

Bryce looked at Leah with one eyebrow raised.

Wow, you are starving. It's like you are eating for two.

Leah looked at Bryce and said, "I am making up for lost time."
"And you know hospital food is not all that great."

With a gentle touch, she placed her hand on her abdomen and whispered a prayer, hoping for a safe and healthy pregnancy. She knew she needed to confirm her suspicions.

Just before Bryce left to pick up the food Leah requested, he assisted her to the bathroom. Leah could stand on her own with the assistance of a walker. She moved to the edge of the bed and took hold of her walker, pausing to prepare herself before standing up. It felt good to stretch her legs.

Leah took her time as she made her way to the bathroom. She stopped to look in the bag that was on the chair. Her first thought was, what has Bryce purchased now? She looked inside, and there were clothes and a note from Anya. Leah read the message and could only smile.

Bryce walked behind Leah as she entered the bathroom.

Leah insisted that she would be fine on her own. If she needed anything, she would pull the call light for help. Bryce left to pick up the food Leah had requested. Leah showered and made it back to bed on her own. Once she was settled, she called for her nurse. The voice on the other end advised that her nurse would arrive shortly.

Hi, Ms. Bernard. My name is Cassie, and I'll be your nurse. How can I help you? Cassie, when I arrived at the hospital, the doctor ordered a pregnancy test, but I never heard the results. Can you check and see if the test was done? If so, can you give me the results? Yes, Ms. Bernard, the doctor did order the test. Bryce walked in just as Cassie was about to give Leah the results. Ms. Bernard, I can come back with that answer if you like. That will be fine, Cassie thanks.

Bryce wondered what the nurse meant when she said she would be back with that answer. He set the bag of food on the table and went into the bathroom to wash his hands.

Leah, is everything OK? Yes, why do you ask? I was curious as to what the nurse meant. When she said she would be back with that answer.

It was nothing; I wanted to know if the doctors had made their rounds and to see if I was being released anytime soon. I am ready to sleep in my bed in my house with my man.

Bryce hugged Leah and said," We will be home soon, enjoying our time together."

Leah could only think we may turn out to be three.

She knew she had a decision to make to either tell Bryce about her suspicion.

Or keep it to herself until she knew for sure.

Leah knew a lot was riding on this.

CHAPTER 26

KIDDIE GAMES

The house was silent when Royce returned. He had taken the day off from work. He needed time to think. It had been a week since he gave Anya the letter about the paternity testing, but she had yet to read it; it remained on the kitchen island. Whenever Royce tried to discuss it, Anya would change the subject or say she didn't want to talk. Royce couldn't continue to live in these conditions since they had promised each other that there would be no secrets between them.

Royce attempted to contact Kane multiple times without success. Eventually, he would have to call Bria, putting his feelings aside for Mia's sake. Before calling Bria, Royce sought advice from a neutral party. Just as he was about to hang up, a voice answered.

UNMASK

Hello, it has been a while since we last spoke. How are you, Royce? Not so great, Mr. Overton. So, you say. Remember, you are talking with someone who has been around a few years. What's on your mind? Royce explained his ordeal surrounding Bria. Before Royce could finish the story, Mr. Overton interrupted him.

Royce, we have become very close over this last year, and I consider you as a grandson. I am going to be very frank with you. You were being irresponsible in your actions. I understand that you were grieving the loss of your wife, but it doesn't excuse it. Your responsibility now is to seek the truth surrounding the paternity of this child.

Do you plan on being with Anya? Yes, Royce said. Then you must talk with Anya because if this child is proven to be yours, Anya will also be a part of their life. So, you don't have time to play kiddie games and wait to see when Anya will read the letter. You have potentially missed out on over a year of this child's life. And to be honest, Royce, if you know women like I do, Anya has probably read the letter and is now processing the information.

Royce, you have no more time to be idle. Your time is now. You can lose what you have been fighting for if you don't move now. And the question is, what are you fighting for?

After speaking to Mr. Overton, Royce gained a new perspective. And he needed that stern, no-objective talk with him. The question that needed to be answered is, what am I fighting for? Royce knows he loves Anya but owes it to himself and Mia to find out if she is his.

Royce redialed Kane's number. The call went to voicemail. He silently prayed before he reached out to Bria. He needed to stay calm and remember that this was not about him but Mia. The phone rang several times before Bria answered.

Hello, who is this?

It's Royce. How did you get this number? Bria asked.

That is not important. I need to know why I am being asked to take another paternity test when the last one indicated that I was not Mia's father. Is there something that I am missing?

Bria said sarcastically, "There could be."

What does that statement mean?

Just take the test, and you will find out.

What games are you playing? You are playing Russian Roulette with not only my life but Mia.

Don't you dare question what I am doing for my daughter? Bria screamed. You have no idea what my life has been like. It is time that you do. Bria hung up the phone without warning.

Royce was puzzled by the hatred in Bria's tone. He now knew what Bryce meant when he said. "Hurt people hurt people." It was never his intention to hurt Bria. Royce realizes he has been selfish and irresponsible in his actions with Bria. And the only one who is suffering is Mia. Mr. Overton is right. It is time to stop playing these kiddie games.

Anya arrived home and was surprised when she opened the door and Royce sat on the couch.

Hello, how was your day? Royce asked. It was busy. How was yours? I spoke with Bria. Oh, you did, Anya said. And how did that go? It did not. She hung up on me. But before she did, she suggested I retake the paternity test.

Anya, I know you read the letter. We need to talk about this. I need to know what you are thinking and feeling and, more importantly, if we will be together if the test reveals that I am Mia's father.

I acknowledge that I did read the letter. Anya replied. And I agree that we must have an honest conversation about the current situation.

Royce sensed an attitude from Anya and anticipated that this would be a difficult conversation.

Royce could hear Mr. Overton's voice echoing, "What are you fighting for."

CHAPTER 27

SURPRISE

Chris stayed up late reviewing his notes for today's hearing. He also examined the case files provided by Loren. Not only was the common theme human trafficking, but all of the victims Dominque represented were of Latin descent from Cuba. That could not be coincidental. It was eight when Chris arrived at the courthouse, and it was rather busy for a Friday. Typically, it is busier Monday through Thursday. He parked his car directly in front of the entrance to the building, allowing him to see when Dominique arrived. Just before nine, Chris spots Dominique pulling into the parking lot. He watches her as she exits the vehicle and approaches the building. Chris quickly gets out of his car and rushes before she enters.

Good morning, Ms. Sanchez. Do you have a minute to talk? Good morning, Mr. Calloway. I am running late. Can you call the office and schedule an appointment with my secretary? What I need to say can be done right now. Chris opens the door for Dominique.

Sure, we can walk and talk, Chris said. Bria Gregory's attorney called, concerned about Bria and Mia's welfare and whereabouts. When did you last speak with Mr. White? I spoke with him last week. Did he mention speaking with Bria? No, it did not come up during our conversation. Also, I haven't received the medical records supporting your claim that Mr. White cannot conceive a child. Lastly, I had a boatload of case files dropped on my desk with your name on them. But what shocked me was that they had nothing to do with family law. It has more to do with the human trafficking of women from Cuba. It is ironic that in this case you are working on, the mother was also involved in a case where there was suspicion of the same thing,

Now, Ms. Sanchez, that is not coincidental. And please understand that I did not graduate from law school at the top of my class because I was handsome. I look forward to hearing from you, and please have the medical records and the evidence that indicates the tampering of samples occurred when Mr. Blackmon submitted his. Dominque remained standing there as Chris walked away. He knows that he has Dominque thinking as to what his next move would be.

Chris knows he needs to find out whether there is a connection between Bryce and the mislabeling of the samples at Coventry Memorial Hospital lab. He was so caught up with the incident at the hospital that he never thought to call the private diagnostic clinic to confirm if they had any affiliation with Coventry. He had Loren call the clinic and ask to speak with the regional operational director. The director was unwilling to deny or agree to whether they had any affiliations with Coventry. Loren reported that Mr. Richard Willis was rude and hung up on her. One thing that Chris did not play about was being disrespectful and rude.

After receiving the information, Chris contacted Ursula at the hospital to inquire if she knew anything more. Ursula informed him that a few private diagnostic clinics had terminated their partnership with Coventry after it was revealed that there was tampering with multiple samples at the central lab. She also confirmed that samples that may have been involved in the mislabeling were collected from March 31 to April 8. Chris recalled that Royce was supposed to have the test two weeks after Mia's birth on March 18, which he remembers because it was his mother's birthday.

Chris arrived at the office the following day and confirmed that Royce had his sample collected on April 3rd. Chris cautiously approached the situation as there was a strong possibility that Royce was among the mislabeled samples. He needed to let Royce know sooner rather than later. He walked down the hall to Royce's office, and the light was still off, which was an obvious indication that he had not made it in.

Chris couldn't imagine the emotional rollercoaster Royce was on. He had a father who chose not to take an active role in their lives and knew he was his child. This left Chris with unanswered questions and unbearable pain. He pulled out a piece of paper from his desk drawer given to him by the officer after Daniel's unexpected visit, still unable to bring himself to call Daniel "father." He analyzed every word. Daniel's writings were similar to how Chris wrote his. How could someone who shares your name be a stranger to you? Chris realized that just because we share the same DNA doesn't mean we are family. It just means we are related.

It was midday when Chris decided to take a break. He couldn't shake this strange feeling that had been lingering about Daniel. However, Daniel had left his number and the address of his residence. He had doubts about Mr. Christopher Daniel Calloway Sr. and felt it was his responsibility to investigate the matter. Chris sought Ashton's help and gave him all the necessary information about Daniel. He requested a thorough and complete investigation that would also delve into Daniel's financial situation. Whatever reason why Daniel decided to come back will be uncovered.

CHAPTER 28

ADIOS

Sal had Jaz clear his calendar for the upcoming week as he prepared to leave for Colorado. He had spoken with Matteo several times since their initial conversation. In their last conversation, Sal instructed Matteo not to mention to anyone, including Abuela and their mother, that he would be traveling to Colorado.

Jaz walked into Sal's office and handed him his flight itinerary. Thanks, Jaz. No problem, I forgot to ask, would you need a vehicle? No, I will have transportation once I arrive. Also, here are your messages. Let me know if you change your mind about a car.

I will. Thanks again, Jaz.

UNMASK

Sal glanced at the messages. None required immediate attention and could wait until he returned from his trip—especially the ones from Mrs. Fontaine. Jaz buzzed in and advised that Wynston Sinclair was holding on line one. Sal immediately picked up the phone. I hope you have some information for me. Wynston Sinclair was Sal's attorney for over five years and had an impeccable, no-nonsense reputation.

Well, hello, Salvatore; it is good to talk with you too. Sal laughed because he knew that Wynston was all bark, no bite. The outside world saw her as this aggressive, high-price attorney who could cut you down with one look. But Sal knew better. I am doing okay, but it would be better if you had some good news.

I do have some good and bad news to share with you. I enlisted a private investigator to travel to Canada in the hopes of finding the whereabouts of Selena. The PI visited the hospital listed on the birth certificate you provided. He spoke to someone in medical records who indicated they did not have a record of Selena Marie Redmon giving birth that day. So, he asked if a document showed anyone with the last name of De La Cruz or Santos. They again stated no. But the registrar did say there was a record of an individual who had given birth under an alias on that day.

The registrar advised typically, this happens when someone is in hiding due to a domestic issue or a celebrity who wants to keep their affairs out of the public eye.

In addition, birth certificates are sometimes issued even though they do not feature the name of a parent. This is because, in many countries, while it is mandatory to register a birth, the certificate can be formalized within one year from the date the baby is born. The registrar also suggested checking vital statics and seeing if the birth mother submitted a revised copy of the birth record. Because these records are public, the PI was able to find a birth certificate with:

Female- Ava Marie Redmond-Shuster
DOB- May 17, 1983
Place of Birth: Home
Mother-Selena Marie Redmond
Age 24
DOB: May 16, 1959

The record still did not list a father but provided more information than we had initially. The PI was able to locate an address for Selena, but when he arrived at the residence, the homeowners advised no one lived there by that name. The PI was unconvinced that the owner was truthful, so he was surveilling the property.

What I need from you is a photo of Selena so that I can get it to the PI. Sal thanked Wynston and immediately called Lou to get a copy of the picture she had of Selena. Sal received the photo from Lou and forwarded it to Wynston. He was ecstatic by the news that he had received.

However, he was not canceling his trip to Colorado because he believed that there was something that his family was keeping from him.

Sal had finally arrived home after picking up his dry cleaning and grabbing some food. He still had a few tasks to complete before leaving for Colorado. Jaz had given him a list of properties to review and some more messages before leaving for the day. He sent a copy of his flight itinerary to Matteo via email and text message. He requested that Jaz book his flight for six in the morning to allow him enough time to inspect Uncle Diego's house before anyone else arrived.

Sal completed his tasks, which included reviewing the list of investment properties, responding to emails, and packing before retiring to bed. It was already late - 10 p.m. As he was about to shut down his computer, he received an email from Jacob Realty and Investment Corporation, a company he had not heard of before. Sal exercised caution because he had previously been hacked and had sensitive data compromised due to a virus embedded in an email. He conducted a quick search to verify the existence of the company. The company was legitimate. He was able to locate additional information on the company via their website. The owner and CEO was Asher Emerson Jacobs. Sal did not recognize the name and was sure he had not done business with him or the company. So, he deleted the email and headed to bed. Sal arrived at Denver International Airport ten minutes before the scheduled time. He confirmed with Matteo last night that he had received the flight details and would pick him up when he landed.

He deboarded the plane and walked from the terminal to retrieve his luggage at baggage claims. Sal noticed how quiet it was, with only a handful of passengers waiting to board their flights. The stillness of the surroundings made it easier for him to hear the sound of his footsteps echoing on the polished floors. Finally, he arrived at baggage claim and checked the overhead monitors to verify which conveyor belt his luggage would come on.

Sal retrieved his cell phone from the holder attached to his belt. He powered the device on and had a text from Matteo.

"I am outside in a grey Tahoe," Sal replied with a thumbs-up emoji.

The red siren blared, "Passengers arriving on flight 1307 from Miami, Florida, you can retrieve your baggage on carousel number three."

Sal grabbed his luggage and went outside in search of Matteo. The coolness of the air was a welcome reprieve from the humidity he had left only hours ago in Miami. He spotted his brother as soon as he walked out the doors. Sal had not seen him in over a year because his job had him working in their satellite office in Japan.

Sal and Matteo inherited their muscular build and hazel eyes from their father, who stood at six foot two inches and weighed approximately one hundred and eighty-five pounds. However, they both shared their mother's complexion and dark hair. As Sal approached Matteo, he couldn't help but notice his striking resemblance to their father. Sal was used to seeing Matteo on Skype or FaceTime. There is nothing like being able to touch and see him in person. The brothers embraced one another before getting in the truck.

During the hour and ten-minute drive to Colorado Springs, the brothers caught up on recent events. Sal expressed his admiration for the new facial hair that Matteo was growing, and Matteo, in turn, teased Sal about the grey he noticed in his hair. Matteo talked extensively about his travel and his love for his job. Sal could see how he stuck out his chest as he spoke about the different projects he was assigned to and the impact that he was making. Sal could only smile and beam with pride for the accomplishments that he had made in such a short period.

Sal updated Matteo on the latest developments as they arrived at the ranch's north gate. Both men got up, and Sal took a moment to take in the scenic views of Pike Peak, which was visible in the distance. He remembers as a child, Uncle Diego would say that the tops of the mountain range were filled with ice cream, and if we were good, he would take us, and we could have all the ice cream we wanted. Sal had many fond memories as a child growing up on the ranch.

Matteo drove down a winding road and passed lush greenery for another ten minutes after opening the gate to reach Uncle Diego's house. The house was nestled in the heart of a densely wooded area, surrounded by tall trees and wildlife. At first glance, it could be mistaken for an abandoned property, but they could see the well-maintained ranch as they approached.

The A-frame-style house stood tall and proud, beckoning them to come closer. The open-concept layout of the house featured high ceilings and an angled roofline, which added to the house's grandeur. But what Sal loved most were the floor-to-ceiling windows that allowed natural sunlight to flood the home, providing breathtaking views of the surrounding hills and valleys. As Matteo had mentioned, it appeared as if someone had been still living in the home. Food was in the refrigerator, and the stove was still warm as if someone had just turned it off. Sal asked, "Do you think Abuela has allowed someone to rent the house?"

No, Matteo replied.

Sal suggested that they began looking for any paperwork that could give any clues to the whereabouts of Selena and Lou's unidentified father.

Sal began in the primary bedroom. He looked through every drawer and combed the closet with a fine-tooth comb. After two hours of searching the home interior, the brothers meet in the living room.

Where would someone put important documents or items for safekeeping?

Matteo said out loud. The obvious place would be a safe or at the bank, but they knew their uncle probably did have an account. They both said in unison under the mattress.

They immediately went into each bedroom, removed the mattress from the beds, and came up empty. Sal and Matteo remained at the house for another four hours before calling it a day. The brothers planned to return to the house and search again in the morning.

Matteo had secured the house as Sal got into the vehicle. Walking from the house to the truck, he noticed fresh footprints leading up to the window. Once Matteo got in, Sal made mention of what he had discovered. Sal suggested that they change the locks when they returned. It was evident that someone had been staying at the house since Uncle Diego had died.

The next day, Sal returned to the house alone because Matteo had an important business meeting that he needed to attend. He stopped at the local hardware store and picked up the replacement locks and a surveillance camera. He also purchased some tools and a ladder. Sal had noticed that several lights were out throughout the house and needed to be replaced.

Sal had spoken to Wynston last night, and she advised that the PI had sent her photos of a woman leaving the residence who resembled Selena, but he was not sure it was her because she wore sunglasses and a hat. Sal asked that those photos be sent to him. He had made it to the house. As Sal opened the door to the house, the light was on in the primary bedroom, and the water in the shower was on. Sal quickly and quietly proceeded to the kitchen and removed a knife from the drawer. He walks swiftly to the bedroom, not realizing what he would find on the other side of the door when he opened it.

CHAPTER 29

NEW BEGINNINGS

Sebastián had just arrived back at the hotel. He had arranged to meet Alex in the lobby at six. They had planned to have dinner together and explore the city. Seemingly out of nowhere, Sebastián began to feel a sense of unease and nervousness. He couldn't quite put his finger on the reason for his apprehension. After all, it was a friendly gesture of hospitality between colleagues, not a romantic date. He knew he was being ridiculous and tried to shake off the feeling.

It was still early in Bangkok, so Sebastián decided to call Ocean and check in. The phone rang several times before she picked up. Hey Dad! The excitement in Ocean's voice made Sebastián's heart sing. Hi, baby girl. How are things going in Bangkok?

Dad, Thailand is amazing. The weather is excellent. Did you know there are only three seasons here: summer, rain or monsoon, and winter? No, I did not.

Have you been able to go sightseeing? Yes, we went on a floating and train market tour. I was able to visit Damnoen Saduak and the waterfalls at Kanchanaburi Erawan. It was so cool, Dad. I got to go to the elephant rescue center too.

Baby girl, it sounds like you are enjoying yourself immensely. I am. Is your mom there? Yes, hold on, let me get her.

Mom, it's Dad, Sebastián could hear Ocean say. Can you put your dad on speakerphone? Yes, Ocean replied.

Hey Sebastián. Hello, I did not want much, Marisa; just checking in. It sounds like you are busy. I dropped the screw to my glasses on the floor, and I was trying to find it.

Sebastián laughed, how many times has the screw popped out of the frame? Too many times to count. It is time to retire the frame. I keep saying you are an undercover hoarder.

Sebastián and Marisa chatted for another fifteen minutes. Marisa filled him in on the assignment and how amazing Bangkok was. Marisa did not ask about his work, only how he was doing. Before hanging up, Marisa said," You sound tired and need to rest."

UNMASK

I know; once I finish what needs to be done here in France, I will, Sebastián replied.

Sebastián heard the concern in her voice. He has been working around the clock since arriving. This case was physically and mentally exhausting. He rose from the chair he was sitting in, opened the door to his room, placed the DO NOT DISTURB sign on the knob, removed his clothes, and napped. A loud knock on the door startled Sebastián from his sleep. He looked around the room, and it was completely dark. There was another knock, which was much louder than the previous one. Sebastián jumped up and opened the door, thinking there was some emergency in the hotel.

It was Alex! She handed him the DO NOT DISTURB sign that had fallen to the floor when Sebastián had opened the door.

Alex could hear Sebastián asking if everything was okay. But her eyes were fixated on his shoulder's broadness and the definition of his muscles. Not to mention how his gray eyes' seemed to change as he talked. She had no clue that he was hiding all of that under those clothes.

Sebastián gently shook Alex by the shoulder, and she realized that she had been staring.

I am sorry, Alex said; I have been calling your room for over twenty minutes. I thought something was wrong when I did not see you in the lobby at six. Sebastián realized that he had overslept. And he was standing at the door in only his boxers. I am so sorry, Alex; let me shower, get dressed, and meet you downstairs in forty-five minutes. That is if you still want to go.

Alex nodded in agreement, turned, and walked toward the elevator.

Sebastián was showered and dressed and in the lobby at seven. Alex had made dinner reservations at The New World Smoke, an American-inspired barbecue restaurant. The ride was quiet. And each time Sebastián would ask Alex a question, she would answer but not look in his direction. He figured it was due to earlier. The car came to a stop in front of the restaurant. Sebastián needed to say something.

Hey, Alex, is everything okay? You have been quiet ever since we left the hotel. Yes, I am good. Please accept my apologies for earlier. I overslept and did not realize I was not fully clothed when I opened the door. I don't want that to ruin our evening. No, it doesn't Alex answered. I was just caught off guard, that is all. And became worried when you did not respond to the calls. Again, my apologies; I did not realize how exhausted I was. No more apologies; we are good, mate. Let's get some food. We have a tour of the city once we finish our meal.

The brisket and Cole slaw were good, but nothing like Mr. Thomas's pulled pork sliders and baked beans. Alex ordered a slab of ribs with fries and barbecue on the side. The conversation picked up after our talk. But Sebastián could tell there was a sense of disconnect from Alex.

Alex took Sebastián on a two-hour guided bus tour of the city. There were stops at the Place Bellecour, Basilica de Notre Dame, and breathtaking views of the Rhone. They were allowed to get off the bus and purchase items from the vendors in the Vieux Lyon district of the city.

Alex was the perfect tour guide. You could easily see she was as fascinated with the views just as Sebastián was. She began to come around and talk more, which is what Sebastián wanted to see. It dawned on him that Alex had shut down because she was embarrassed.

Sebastián found himself staring at Alex from a distance. He noticed that when she laughed, she would hold her stomach. Or, when thinking, she squints her eyes and bites her lower lip. Something he found to be sexy. They had come to the last stop on the tour. Sebastián helps Alex off the bus.

They walked back toward the restaurant where they had parked the car. Their conversation was still upbeat as they drove, but she immediately stopped speaking as Alex approached the hotel. There was an awkward silence, as if they both were thinking of what to do or say next.

Sebastian noticed that Alex was biting her lower lip. He knew that she was thinking. The silence broke when Alex said, "Sebastian, I think you are an amazing man. I've had such a wonderful evening with you and wish that it did not have to end. I don't want to complicate an already volatile situation." And what situation is that? Sebastian asked. The one that will have us regretting the following day. Sebastián fully understood Alex's statement.

Two days passed, and the team was in the final planning stages of Operation Styles. The group met that morning, and everyone was in place. Gear on and guns strapped. The CI indicated Styles was scheduled to land at eight at Charles de Gaulle airport that evening. Chief Inspector Wellington had agents stationed in the arriving terminal and baggage claims. But something in Sebastián's gut told him that Styles would not be on that flight. Sebastián radioed Chief Inspector Wellington to inform him of his suspicion. The response was not from Wellington but from Mr. Baxter. He instructed Sebastián to call him.

Sebastián advised Mr. Baxter of his suspicion. His suspicion was confirmed. He spoke with Detective Reynolds moments later. He had received information that Styles had been tipped off. However, the shipment was still going to be delivered as planned. The transport route had changed, and now was on a private luxury liner scheduled to dock at Quai Claude Bernard at midnight. Sebastián conveyed this information to Mr. Baxter. Baxter advised it was a five-hour commute by car. They could only make it there in time by helicopter, which they had at their disposal.

Mr. Baxter updated Chief Inspector Wellington on the new information and instructed him to continue as planned. Agents would stay in place in their assigned locations, and he would be heading to Quai Claude Bernard with Special Agent Moreau, Collins, and two more Interpol Agents who had been assigned to that region recently.

Mr. Baxter needed to take the necessary precautions because there was a mole among them. The team was transported by van to an undisclosed location, where Mr. Baxter briefed them on the plan for tonight. He also had made contact with law enforcement in the area. Meanwhile, Chief Inspector Wellington confirmed that Styles was not on the flight but had a person in custody who fit the description of someone with ties to Styles.

After an impromptu meeting, Sebastián took a moment to clear his mind and focus on the task at hand. He closed his eyes and held onto his dad's dog tags, the only thing he had that belonged to him. During his last visit with Ja'Nae, she gave him the tags. Sebastián hoped that gripping the tags tightly would draw his father's energy and strength, which he needed at that moment.

Sebastián had noticed that Alex had not said anything since the group stopped at this location. He figured she was clearing her mind as he had done moments before. The van began to move again. Mr. Baxter informed them that we would arrive at the helipad in thirty minutes.

UNMASK

Sebastián knew that the fate of his career hung in limbo.

The team assembly at Part-Dieu train station thirty minutes outside the port. Angelo met them, their contact from the local police, and he confirmed the names of the passengers on Le' Nubian Luxury Liner. Desmond Arrington was not on the list, but Rex Slaughter was. Mr. Baxter requested that the names of the remaining passengers be given to Riff so he could verify their identity and if they had any connections to Styles. Mr. Baxter had Alex ride with Lugo and Tess, the other Interpol agents, so that she could give the case details. Sebastián rode with Riff, Angelo, and Mr. Baxter to the port.

Riff identified three other individuals on the passenger list who were positively identified as having a connection with Styles. Riff also advised that a small child was confirmed as a passenger signed in under Rex Slaughter's name. That information changed the dynamics of the plans. Riff provided the team with photos of all suspects.

Lugo, Riff, and Sebastián were enlisted to be porters. This would allow them access to the boat when it docked. Angelo called for additional backup at the port and the surrounding area.

The ship slowly pulled into the port. Lugo, Riff, and Sebastián had positioned themselves on the dock as the boat stopped. The anchor was dropped, and the passengers began to deboard. Sebastián was able to hear the traffic in the earpiece that was affixed to his right ear. Angelo radioed, announcing he had eyes on Rex Slaughter and two other suspects, one of whom appeared to be carrying a child. The third suspect had not been spotted.

Sebastián swiftly moved in as Rex made his way down the catwalk.

Good evening, Sir; please allow me to assist you and your campion with your luggage. Sebastián could see Alex approaching. He began conversing with Styles and the female carrying the child.

Madam, you appear to be tired. I can have another porter come and assist you with the child. Sebastián called out to Alex. Hey, Alex, would you help this passenger and her child? She is exhausted from the trip. Sebastián continued conversing with Styles, and suddenly, gunshots rang out from inside the boat. Sebastián took hold of Styles while Alex did the same with the female. Tess and Angelo had made their way to Sebastián and Alex and escorted Styles and the female with the child to a car waiting at the end of the pier. Riff radioed and indicated the third suspect had taken two passengers hostage. He had overheard another passenger say he saw several unmarked police cars as they pulled into the port.

Sebastián and Alex took cover at the top of the catwalk near the door. They cautiously entered the vestibule. They could hear talking from the lower deck of the boat. Alex motioned that she would take the stairs on the far end of the ship while Sebastián took the stairs on the opposite end. Several minutes later, gunshots were heard again. Mr. Baxter radioed out for their status, and neither one responded.

CHAPTER 30

ROUND TWO

Anya gazed out of the picture window in the guest room as raindrops started falling. She had been sleeping there for the past two nights. Upon returning home after spending the day at the river, she was taken aback to find Royce home early.

She had rehearsed what she would say to Royce when she saw him. As a woman, we have this built-in radar called intuition. Anya knew in her heart that regardless of whether or not the paternity test proved that Royce was or was not the father, Bria was not going anywhere.

Anya thought the conversation had started well. Royce greeted her and asked about her day, to which she responded with the same question. However, Royce's tone changed when he suggested that he knew she had read the letter and that he wanted to see if she would stay with him if Mia were his. This made Anya take a step back and assess the situation.

Anya had always been sure she would not leave Royce if Mia turned out to be his child. However, the thought of Royce co-parenting with Bria was a matter that required careful consideration on her part. Soon after, Royce surprised Anya by disclosing that he had spoken to Bria, catching Anya off guard. Yet again.

When asked what was said in the conservation with Bria, Royce said it was brief, and Bria implied that it would be in his best interest that he retook the paternity test. That statement did not sit well with Anya.

First, what did Bria mean by that?

Second, how many times had Royce communicated with Bria?

Third, how long has Royce known about retaking the test?

Royce's answer to the first two questions felt like there was some truth in what he was saying. But when he answered the last question, he said he received it the day he had given it to Anya.

Anya was mortified that Royce would insult her intelligence by lying to her. There was no way he had received the letter on that day. She remembered the postmark on the envelope was in March, and the paternity test was scheduled on April 16th.

She told herself not to jump to conclusions. Let it play out.

But what do you say when the words spoken are not true? And all you hear in your mind is you are competing with someone who has given your man something you cannot—his first child.

The back-and-forth dialogue led to no actual resolution. Everything Royce said had a ring of inconsistency. Anya wanted to believe that she was being emotional. And this was a misunderstanding.

Anya had scheduled an appointment today at 11:00 a.m. with Dr. Summerton because she was experiencing nose bleeds and headaches. Nothing as severe as migraines. But she was concerned and wanted to make sure. Anya believed that the nose bleeds and the recent stress was triggering the headaches. She wishes she could talk with Leah, but that was not an option for obvious reasons. So, she also scheduled a video visit with Eileen at 3:00.

She showered, dressed, and went to the kitchen to make something quick to eat. She wanted to be out the door before Royce left for work. After their discussion last night, Royce alluded that he had no more time to play kiddie games and knew what he needed to fight for. And apparently, it was not her. Anya no longer wanted anything to eat, so she retrieved her belongings and left.

Once in her vehicle, Anya sat, taking in the beautiful sunrise. She marveled at God in His infinite wisdom. She prayed that she was not overthinking or again placing judgment on both Royce and even Bria. She had never been a parent and could not imagine what they were going through. But deep down in Anya's gut, she knew something was wrong.

Anya stopped to get some gas, a cup of coffee, and a pecan roll. As she pumped her gas, Dr. Summerton's office called and advised they had a cancellation and could come in early if she liked. Anya agreed to the earlier appointment but headed to the office before going.

It was still early, and the only person that would be in at this hour would be Stacie. Stacie had taken on so much since Leah had been away. And not to mention all the other responsibilities she had. When Anya opened the office door, the lights were still off, and the blinds were drawn, which was a clear indication that Stacie had not made it in. She walked to her office and turned on her computer. Anya had 300 unread emails and several messages left on her desk. Anya skimmed through the emails and letters to see if anything stood out and required immediate attention. There were several messages from Terri regarding the property in Miami. Anya made a mental note to call Terri when she left Dr. Summerton's office.

Anya was a little nervous after she checked in. On her last visit, Royce had accompanied her. She knew she needed to keep it together. Dr. Summerton agreed after talking with Anya that the current nose bleeds and headaches could be associated with the stress she was experiencing now. He suggested more self-care days. Anya was relieved, but Dr. Summerton stressed that she keeps a close eye on the nose bleeds if she cannot stop the bleeding, has trouble breathing, or has vomited from swallowing blood to go straight to the hospital for immediate care. Anya scheduled a follow-up visit in a month. Her visit with Eileen went well also; she agreed with Dr. Summerton about self-care and potentially taking a trip to refocus and take inventory of her life and what was important to her.

Royce had called when Anya was on her video visit with Eileen, so she could not answer. He left a voicemail message:

"Anya, the last two weeks have been a nightmare. And I don't think we are on the same page. I am scheduled to take the paternity test next Wednesday. I think it would be best to move out until I get the results. It will allow us time to figure out where we fit into each other's life."

Anya picked up the phone and called Terri and had her scheduled time for her to view the property this weekend. She then called and made a one-way flight reservation to Miami.

CHAPTER 31
BLINDSIDE

Royce decided to go into the office. On the way in, Chris called to check-in. Royce informed him he was scheduled to take the paternity test this Wednesday. Chris, in return, told Dominique and Lydia, who advised that she had spoken with Bria and that she and Mia were safe. When Chris arrived at the office, he could see a shift in Royce's mood. He was not his confident and social self. Chris knows this paternity test is taking a toll on Royce physically and emotionally.

Chris entered Royce's office, closed the door, sat, and said, "We have been friends for a long time, and I know when S##? is bad. You look like a truck ran over you. I cannot imagine what you are going through. But as a child whose father left their life very early, I know that pain.".

I also know what a devoted mother looks like. And someone who loves you unconditionally. And so do you, Royce. Your parents have been and still are present in your life. We may not be blood brothers, but I consider you as one. I will be here to support you however you need me to."

Royce sat silent for a long time. Man, I feel as if this nightmare will never end. I slept with a woman I did not love and am now paying the consequence for a few months of temporary pleasure. I found a woman who makes me a better man. She is everything I could want as a wife and a mother to my children. But these last few weeks have shown me a different side of her. A side that I would not have expected. Was this also something temporary? Chris allowed Royce to talk without interruption. He could see that Royce had been holding on to some unresolved issues that stemmed from the death of Skylar. Chris needed to do everything he could to provide an amicable resolution if Royce was or was not confirmed to be the father. Before ending his conversation with Royce, Chris suggested that he take some time off. Chris did not want to add more salt to the wound and reminded Royce that this was the week he would transfer all his open cases to him in preparation for his move to Miami with Anya.

The medical records finally came in, and the findings indicated that Mr. White did have a vasectomy performed after he married Bria. Not before, as Ms. Sanchez first claimed. The semen analysis suggested that the surgery was not a success. It appears that there was a recanalization of the vas deferens. And Mr. White is capable of conceiving a child. In addition, Chris received information that Lucas was also retested and is awaiting the final results.

Chris replayed the conversation with Ms. Sanchez in his head about the other potential fathers. Was there another father in this equation? Only time will tell. Chris's mother always said," What happens in the dark will come to the light."

****

Royce realized he had unpacked some heavy things in his conversation with Chris. The weight of everything was too much for him to carry any longer. His life was spinning out of control. And the desire to communicate his fears to the woman he loved was slipping away.

As someone who gets paid to defend others, Royce could not articulate what he needed from Anya.

Did he have the right to ask Anya to be an instant mom potentially?

Royce thought about that question for a moment.

He knew that Bria would be difficult to deal with. It was apparent in their last conversation. Was he so invested in being a father that he was losing himself? Or was he holding on to a dream of being a dad to his and Skylar's child?

Royce realized that he fully had not grieved Skylar death. And indeed, not the baby.

Royce needed to process his feelings and the direction he would take. He contacted Jeffrey Woods, the firm's owner, to inform him he would be taking a leave of absence for personal reasons. Mr. Woods had been instrumental in Royce's career and credited him with consistently demonstrating what black excellence looked like. Mr. Woods understood and wished Royce the best. And ensured him he would always have a place with Woods, King, and Jackson Law Firm.

Royce called Stephen and informed him of his decision. Royce ensured Stephen he would still have a job at the firm once he relocated.

Stephen asked Royce what his plans were once he relocated. Royce could not give Stephen a definite answer because he was unsure. Stephen advised that if he ever needed a legal assistant, please don't hesitate to call him. After receiving his instructions from Royce, Stephen asked what he would like for him to do with his belongings in the office.

Royce advised I will have the movers come this weekend to retrieve them. Royce's last day was coming to an end. Stephen, Chris, several of the firm partners, and Loren had come by to say goodbye before they left. Royce stood at the window looking out at the city for the last time. He had no clue what tomorrow would hold. But he was sure he needed to be prepared.

Royce placed a few keepsakes from his desk in a box. He looked around the office before he turned off the light. He removed the engraved name placard and closed the door.

Bryce had called earlier with updates on Leah. Royce could hear the excitement in his voice as he spoke about Leah's progress. Bryce was hopeful that Leah would be released to go home soon. Royce told Bryce he would come by the hospital once he left work.

Royce had not heard from Anya since he left the voicemail message. In his mind, Royce did not expect Anya to call him back. But he hoped she would. Before going to the hospital, Royce made a detour to a place he had not visited in a long time.

Royce parked his vehicle on the side road leading to the entrance of Memorial

Garden Cemetery. This was his first visit since he laid Skylar and their baby to rest. As he slowly walked towards the tree, he felt the weight of the moment hit him. When he reached where Skylar was buried, he saw the bench he had placed diagonally across from the headstone. The bench had been engraved with Skylar's name and the picture of their baby's sonogram. He sat down and read the words engraved on the massive limestone:

"Our Fairytale Ended Way Too Soon. We Had So Much More To See And Do. I Will Not Question Why. As You Are Now With Our Father In Heaven, Rejoicing With Our Bundle Of Joy. Until We Met Again.

Your Loving Husband

Royce."

He embraced the realness of the moment, feeling the weight of his loss and the love he still held for his wife and child.

Royce felt the tears roll down his face. The only way he knew how to release this pain was to yell. He let out a heart-wrenching cry that erupted from the depths of his belly. He falls to his knees, crying uncontrollably. He asked Skylar for forgiveness for not being there to protect her and their baby. And not saying he loved her more. Royce wept until he had nothing left. He was exhausted. As he went to stand, two doves ascended from the sky and came to rest on Skylar headstone. Royce could only smile. He remembered when his grandmother passed away; a dove landed on her coffin as they lowered her into the grave. His mother said, "Your Yay Yay is now in heaven with Pop Pop."

This was Royce's sign that Skylar was now at peace in heaven with their baby.

CHAPTER 32
YOUR INTERPRETATION

Abbey arrived at work and was greeted by her Robyn with a dozen long-stemmed red roses. Abbey's face lit up; she knew it was from Jamerson. They had been spending a lot of time together lately. Jamerson invited Abbey to an art exhibition where one of his friends showcased their artwork. The exhibit was breathtaking, and Abbey witnessed another side of Jamerson and felt a strong connection with him.

Abbey took the glass vase from Robyn and walked to her office. Once in her office, Abbey removed the card and read the message:

Abbey,

I have enjoyed our time together and cannot wait for our next adventure.

Your Friend,

Jamerson

Abbey was not sure how to take the note.

Did Jamerson only see her as his friend?

Did he have a girlfriend?

Or was he married?

Abbey still did not know what Jamerson did for a living, and he had not asked what she did either. Abbey felt as if it was intrusive and did not want to leave an impression that she was a gold digger. She has had several friends involved with married or attached men unbeknown to them. Robyn buzzed in and advised that Anya was on the line.

Thanks, Robyn put her through.

Hi Anya, how are you?

I have seen better days. But I will not complain.

Abbey could detect sadness in Anya's voice. The last time they spoke, she was upbeat about them partnering together and going to see a potential space for the satellite office in Miami.

Are you sure that everything is OK, Anya?

Yes, I am good. Just exhausted. I called today to see if you and your team can meet this Friday.

I will have Robyn confirm and reach out to Stacie with the time. OK, thanks.

How is Leah doing? She is doing well. I spoke with her today. I plan to visit with her later this evening. Please send her my love and well wishes.

I am here if you need to talk Abbey said before Anya released the call.

Abbey had Robyn check her calendar and schedule a meeting with Anya's firm for Friday.

Abbey could not shake the feeling that Jamerson may be involved in a relationship. She GOOGLE Signs That A Man Is Involved Or Married. Jamerson has several characteristics:

He only sees her at certain times of the day or week.

Their dates have been after 7:00 PM and continuously during the week.

He won't tell you his full name or give you many details about where he works.

Abbey did not know Jamerson's last name. But then again, she never asked him either. And to be fair, she chose not to ask him what he did for a living.

Subconsciously, all Abbey had to do was ask.

Abbey closed her door so she could have more privacy.

Abbey dialed Jamerson's number. It rang once, twice, and on the third ring, Jamerson answered.

Good morning Abbey; how are you? I am great. I wanted to call and thank you for the beautiful roses.

You are welcome. I hope you like them.

I do Abbey replied.

I was not sure what color you preferred, but I remembered that while at the exhibit, you mentioned how lovely the floral arrangement was, and they were red long-stemmed roses.

Abbey remembered saying that.

Can I ask you a question, Jamerson? Please know this is not to offend you. Abbey, you can ask me anything you like. I am an open book.

OKAY

What is your full name?

How old are you?

Are you married? Currently seeing anyone. Engaged.

Do you have a job? That you can file taxes on.

Do you have any children on the way? Or any that you are presently paying child support for.

Jamerson laughed, and without hesitation, he answered Abbey's questions.

Jamerson Adolfo Fischer, Fischer is spelled F-I-S-C-H-E-R. I was named after my grandfather, who was German.

I am 33 and will be celebrating a birthday on November 16. That would make me a Scorpio.

I am unmarried and never engaged, but I am currently seeing someone.

I am an airline pilot. And my bookkeeper filed my taxes early. Because I knew I would be out of the country on April 18.

I have no children but would like at least two. But I see my niece every other weekend when her mom has to work.

Can I call you right back Jamerson asked. Sure, Abbey replied.

Abbey felt like a complete fool. She would not be surprised if Jamerson did not call back. She had interrogated him in less than five minutes.

Abbey's phone rang, and it was Jamerson Face Timing her. She was nervous but answered.

I am sorry it was my sister at the door.

Abbey, this is my sister Miranda and my niece Denver.

Hey Abbey, It is a pleasure to put a face to a name finally. Jamie said he was seeing someone special.

Abbey blushed. Are you coming to the get-together this weekend Miranda asked. Abbey did not know how to respond. Jamerson took the phone from his sister. Miranda, I was going to ask her, but you have asked for me. Abbey, do you have any plans this weekend? Yes, I do with you. Perfect, I will pick you up at 10:00 in the morning.

Abbey felt confident enough to put down her guard with Jamerson. But she needed to converse more with Jamerson about having children. Abbey was in that window where she would be at high risk if she became pregnant. She was not going to think about it right now. She needed to figure out what to wear at this function this weekend.

CHAPTER 33

PLUS, ONE

Leah was excited because her doctors were releasing her from the hospital on Friday. Bryce was home rearranging the furniture so she could maneuver downstairs with the walker. Cassie was able to give Leah the results of the pregnancy test when Bryce stepped out of the room. Indeed, Leah was about ten weeks pregnant based on her last menstrual period. She was nervous to tell Bryce because they had not been together that long.

Although they had talked about having children, it was when they first started dating, and it was never discussed again. Leah had spoken to Anya earlier today, and she would come by this evening. Leah had not told Anya either. She wanted Bryce to know first. Cassie had come in to say hello. She was Leah's nurse again tonight. Cassie informed Leah that she had orders for an ultrasound and transportation would be there to pick her up in ten minutes. Leah asked several questions regarding the ultrasound.

So, why am I having the ultrasound?

Cassie smiled and said," It is to measure the size of your baby. And confirm when you are expected to deliver. But most important to make sure the baby is developing as it should."

I am sorry, Cassie, for asking all of these questions. I have never been pregnant, so this is all new to me. It is OK. I understand you have been through a lot. And this is a lot to process. Ms. Bernard, please ask me any questions that you have. That is why I am here. As promised, the transporter arrived to take Leah to her ultrasound. Before leaving, she asked Cassie if Bryce could be escorted to radiology when he returned. Cassie said absolutely.

Leah waited to be called by the technician. Her mind was racing. She was concerned the effects of being on a ventilator would have on the baby. Then, she questioned her ability to be a good mom. She began to cry because she needed her mom. And honestly, she had no idea how Bryce would react when she told him.

The technician called Leah's name and asked her to verify her name and date of birth. Leah complied with the technician's request. She asked Leah a series of questions:

When was your last menstrual?

How many living children do you have?

What is your medical and surgical history?

Have you had any miscarriages or pregnancy complications?

Are you taking any medication?

Leah answered all of the questions. The tech had Leah lay back on the table. She had Leah raise her pajama top. The tech advised that she would need to apply some warm gel to her abdomen. Just as she applied the gel to the wand connected to the ultrasound machine, there was a knock at the door.

The person at the door advised there was a Bryce Blackmon to see Ms. Bernard and asked if it was okay to bring him back.? Yes, Leah said he is the father. Bryce walked in and took a seat next to Leah. Leah could make out what Bryce was thinking or feeling.

The tech slowly ran the wand across Leah's abdomen. She explained that she was taking measurements of the fetus to determine its size and how many weeks Leah was pregnant. Bryce still had not said a word; his eyes were focused on the screen.

Leah couldn't take it anymore; the silence was driving her crazy.

Is everything OK with the baby?

Yes, they are feisty and like to move. So, it is taking me longer to get their measurements.

Leah let out a sigh of relief. Are you able to determine the sex of the baby? No, when you are about 16-20 weeks old, you can return to find out. Based on your last menstrual period, you are about ten weeks pregnant.

The tech gave Leah two sonogram pictures. And advised she will give her time to get cleaned up. The tech handed Leah a warm towel to remove the gel from her abdomen and exited the room..

Leah was cautious and asked Bryce what he was thinking.

I understand that this was not what you were expecting, nor was I. If you want to... Bryce stopped Leah. You never have to question my intention. I love you and this baby. We created this child out of love, and they will be loved.

Bryce let everyone they passed in the hallway to Leah's room know he was going to be a dad. And this beautiful woman here is carrying my baby.

When Bryce and Leah arrived back to the room, Anya was waiting. Leah was so excited to see Anya. She got out of the wheelchair with Bryce's assistance. She hugged Anya so tight that she was not able to breathe.

Hi, Auntie Ya!

She handed Anya the sonogram. I am so happy for you both. When is your due date, Leah? I am about ten weeks, and I am due on October 26.

Royce walked in as Anya was congratulating Leah and Bryce on their news. He was not expecting to see Anya today. He was happy to see her, but her expression did not say the same. Anya chatted with Leah and Bryce until visiting hours had ended. Leah hugged Anya as she was about to leave and whispered.

Are you and Royce OK?

We are fine. I will call you tomorrow.

Anya said goodnight and walked out. Royce soon followed.

Anya was at the elevator when Royce approached. I will be by tomorrow to get some of my things. Anya nodded her head in agreement. Are you going to say anything? Royce asked.

No, everything that needs to be said has been.

Royce could hear Mr. Overton say, "Whatever you are going through, this too shall pass. Trust in the process; your time to love again is coming."

PREVIEW OF UNMASK/ BOOK 4

WORTH FIGHTING FOR

What does the future hold for Anya and Bryce? Will the results of this second paternity test seal the fate of their relationship? Has Bria finally got what she wanted? Or will they have what it takes to fight to keep things together?

Can longtime friend and Attorney Chris Calloway be the key to savaging

UNMASK

Anya and Bryce's relationship? Or does he need support to overcome his childhood traumas? Or will he put it on the back burner to solve a mystery involving Dominique Sanchez, the opposing attorney in Bryce and Bria's ongoing paternity court case?

Sebastián has been given an opportunity to advance in his career. Will this mission propel his career to the next level? Has Sebastián found his next love abroad? Is Alex just someone to take the place of Anya? Or has Sebastián met his match with Alex? Will she be his saving grace?

Sal considers himself a family man, so when his cousin Lou comes to him for assistance locating her parents, will secrets from the past have him reevaluating the meaning of family? Or will a chance encounter with. Realtor A.J. caused him to abandon his wild ways and consider settling down.

Abbey is looking for the love that her parents have. Will she find that in Jamerson Fischer? Or does she have a secret admire that she is not aware of? Will the news of Leah and Bryce's bundle of joy be too much for the new couple? Or will it cause them to work that much harder to keep things together since everyone around them is crumbling under the pressure?

Are these relationships worth fighting for? Or should they walk away before more causalities become involved?

Illustration By Anthony L. Wardrett

Words of Wisdom

Unmask is a powerful journey that tells the stories of countless faceless women. As the author, I deliberately gave each woman a voice and a name. Their tales are filled with triumph, obstacles, and sorrow, yet they all share a common thread: the ability to persevere and overcome adversity. As women, we are built to endure and be resilient through life's challenges. We possess the strength to find a way even when it seems impossible. So, let us intentionally lift one another up, encourage each other, and empower and motivate one another to be our best selves.

Dr. Calenthia Yvette Miller

ARE YOU SETTLING, OR ARE YOU SOARING?
THE DIFFERENCE BETWEEN THE TWO IS THAT IT IS UP TO
YOU.